OUTERSPACE
AND
BEYOND

Mars

Dooma

Mercury

Sol

Earth

BY: HUGH Y. RAYMENT

Order this book online at www.trafford.com
or email orders@trafford.com

Most Trafford titles are also available at major online book retailers.

Printed in Victoria, BC, Canada.

ISBN: 978-1-4269-1577-2

*Our mission is to efficiently provide the world's finest, most comprehensive
book publishing service, enabling every author to experience success.
To find out how to publish your book, your way, and have it available
worldwide, visit us online at www.trafford.com/10510*

Trafford rev: 12/28/2009

 www.trafford.com

North America & international
toll-free: 1 888 232 4444 (USA & Canada)
phone: 250 383 6864 ♦ fax: 812 355 4082

<u>Forward</u> by A.F. Rayment

Of Hugh Rayment I delight to relate some tales of his story telling in early years and later times that have amused our listening ears. Well I remember in early times we tuck into our parents bed – the whole six of us led by myself, the eldest, followed by sister Joyce, and then Hughie, Alfred, Ken, and Tom My sister would say, "Hughie, Tell us a story of ----". He would tell a version oft told but with lots of embellishment to brighten up the tale. Some of these stories may be termed as outrageous. That was when we were under twelve years old.

Now, in later years, after the battle days of WW2, he would be relating bitter tales in his search of me, a prisoner of war in Germany. In the midst of his tale a loud stern voice from my mother, "Hughie"!! meaning she had overheard an embellishment she was skillful at detecting. So the story was told in basic truth but with some embellishments to make it the more interesting. Now my fellow readers, see if you can pick out the embellishments found in this tale of all tales, "Outer Space and Beyond". "Is it all that outrageous"?

Fred Rayment

Acknowledgment

To Fred for his flattering forward and his witty remarks and for remembering those days and events of over seventy years ago. I extend my gratitude to Miss Liz Allerdice and Miss Arnold, the art teachers at Seaton High School for guiding one of her students, Grayson Kashino in providing the graphics and illustrations for this book. He had to reach into the future and imagine what his subjects would look like a thousand years hence. My doctor, Dr. Donald Smith for pulling me through two heart attacks during the production of this book.

I extend a very sincere thank you to my wife Elsie for putting up with the many hours I spent in the computer room while putting this story to print. I also thank my daughter Lynda for proof reading my script and picking out a few typos and persuading me to put some of my statements into the proper perspective to suit modern times.

A very special thank you to my daughter Judy Rayment-Tait for helping me through the final edit.

Chapter One

This story records events that start out on the campus of a mid western university I shall call Hummer University somewhere on the planet Earth. All characters' names in this story are fictitious to protect the innocent. Any similarity to anyone I know is purely coincidental. The time is 3110AD.

A group of science students got together every Saturday to discuss a topic of common interest; space, time, and the universe. Astrology was their passion; a world of space travel and discovery. Great advances had been made in space technology over the past century Space travel had become commonplace in vehicles that moved twenty times faster and were capable of travel far into space, even beyond our solar system. The propulsion system allowed a very gentle lift-off so that the astronauts felt little discomfort during their ride into space.

Life on Earth showed little difference from the twenty first century. Wars over differences in religious beliefs still raged on. A quarter of the population still was living below the poverty line. Distribution of the necessities of life had not improved very much. Education had made great strides and yet people had not learned to live together in peace. Politicians still struggled for power and the almighty dollar still ruled. There was plenty for all but greed took precedence and, as is often said, "The rich became richer and the poor became poorer". Pollution of our atmosphere, rivers, and lakes was a major concern and still there was disagreement on what to do about it. It would take huge efforts and money from all the countries of the world to save the planet from certain destruction. At least this was the opinion of scientists around the world. Global warming was threatening all forms of life in the sea, in the air, as well as on the land. All these things seemed to be ignored by the majority of people. As the saying goes, "They just buried their heads in the sand", and hoped the problems would go away.

These were the problems that faced our group of young scientists. They wondered how all the changes needed to improve matters could be accomplished. They all agreed that somehow answers could be found in outer space. Could there be another inhabited planet in our solar system? Perhaps there was such a planet that traveled the same orbit as Earth and at the same speed and therefore could not be seen from Earth because it was always hidden behind the sun. They reasoned that the UFO's seen on Earth were from somewhere out there and that their theory may hold the answer. All members of the group were anxious and willing to train as astronauts and explore our solar system to try to confirm their beliefs. This of course had been stated as impossible by some scientists who said that such a planet would upset the equilibrium of our solar system. Dauntless our group held to their beliefs and decided that, as soon as they graduated, they would go ahead with their plans.

In order to accomplish their mission it would be necessary to have certain specialists in their crew. Their first officer [captain] would have to learn all there was to know about the new high speed space vehicles and indeed take part in the design of their craft before taking such a long journey. Bill Williams was select6ed for this job.

The next post to fill was space navigator and Sally Post, being an expert mathematician, volunteered for that position. They would need a dietician and a cook to plan and prepare the food. Jim Bolder and Mary Swan were confident that between them they could fill the spot. Very importantly they would have to have a doctor on board and Tom Morgan would be able to complete his master's degree in time to fill that position. In their discussions they decided that they should have a person who was good at deciphering language, a linguist. Who else was there to choose but Harry Good? He was quite fluent in five languages and also had spent several years teaching languages in a local high school before getting interested in space science. They also needed someone to keep the house in order. Jane Silver took on that job. She would also keep track of supplies and see that all the necessities of daily living were on board. After all they could be away for up to five years. It must be understood that this space ship had to be very large in order to carry enough supplies to sustain a crew of ten for that long. Fred Wong volunteered to look after the ships heating and cooling systems. He would also be responsible for taking air samples if they were to land on another planet. Betty Simms specialized in geology and would take and analyze soil samples. Toni Janske had studied biology and genetics since her first year in high school. So this was the crew of the space ship they chose to name Moonbeam. Captain Bill Williams was quite a religious man. In earlier days he had thought about going into the ministry but got caught up in the intrigue of the prospective space mission. None of the crew would be leaving spouses behind, as they were single and had no children.

The preparation time before departure would be at least

one year. Moonbeam had to be completed and the crew had to be trained for space travel. Clothing had to be fitted and of course the food supply had to be prepared and placed in storage prior to finally loading the ship. All the storage compartments had to be specifically arranged so that the ship was in reasonable balance for the take-off.

The crew decided to keep this venture secret from the press for the time being because there were many skeptics ready to ridicule and complain about public research money being spent on such a mission. Even some of the government officials had some doubt about the validity of it. There was a certain amount of fear of the survival of the space ship which cost millions to build, to say nothing for the safety of the crew. The construction workers and the technicians were well aware of this record breaking journey about to take place and they put their hearts and souls into the project as though they themselves would be on board. They called Moonbeam their baby and so it was that this beautiful ship took shape.

The days and months passed and the crew was having a ball taking their space training and toning up to go. They had to take a trip in a smaller ship as part of their training. This was a relatively short trip of five orbits of the earth that also included a space walk by the captain and the tech. It was also important that each member of the crew was familiar with and knew how to operate every piece of research equipment as well as full operation of Moonbeam. With each passing day excitement rose in all of them.. The anticipation of their historic lift-off and their stringent training occupied every minute of their days.

At last the day of graduation from space flight school came and all of the crew was ready to go. All that remained now was to wait for the proper window of time for a safe launch. The moon had to be in the right location of its orbit as did the space station and of course weather conditions could determine the exact time of lift-off. The crew had practiced the drill of getting dressed in their flight gear and getting into their positions on board many times over. In the final hours the ship was fueled up and all was ready to go.

Chapter Two

It is five AM on May 24, 3012. The sun is peeping over the horizon and our crew is dressed and ready to board Moonbeam. Farewells to family and friends had been made at the reception center and the crew had boarded a bus that took them to the launch pad. Upon an order from the launch captain they filed into the ship, each waving a final farewell as they entered. They had fifteen minutes to get settled into their respective positions and the count-down began. As mentioned before, new technology allowed for a gentle ride into space.

As they rose though the stratosphere there was very little noise, just a noticeable feeling of pressure as acceleration pressed them into their seats. Captain Bill Williams checked with navigator Sally Post for their position and he radioed back to control announcing a safe lift-off and that they were on course. Acceleration was very gradual by modern space travel standards. It would take two days to reach top speed. They estimated that it would take about 300 days to reach the far side of the sun. Distance was now measured in days rather than in miles.

The ship was moved into position to be in the exact orbit of Earth. They knew that radio contact would be lost as soon as they passed behind the sun unless they could bounce a signal off another planet. This bit of technology had been discussed but it would have to be tried out by this crew to see if it were possible.

Now the crew had almost a year of travel before them before reaching their proposed destination. Would they find their lost planet? If there were nothing there they would just continue on their orbit and return home to Earth. There was plenty to do as there were millions of heavenly bodies out there to examine through their telescopes. Every observation had to be recorded and photographs had to be taken. Astrologers have mapped the universe as seen from Earth but this was much larger and a golden opportunity to gather accurate information about the universe.

As the ship continued on its way through endless space the crew was rewarded with awesome views through the windows of their craft. Each day Earth became smaller. Continents and oceans became more difficult to identify. They got to see the back side of the moon and do considerable amount of mapping and researching of this amazing sphere in our sky. They experienced radio silence when the moon came between them and Earth. Betty Simms was able to pick up radio reception the rest of the time so that they could get news from home and other entertainment as well. They knew well enough that they would later have to rely upon taped music. Captain Bill ordered the crew to spend only certain hours at work and to take time for relaxation. Dr. Tom Morgan took record of each member's vitals every morning and kept a close watch on the mental health of each one. All crew members were very compatible and for the time being seemed to be one big happy family. After all, what they had to look forward to kept them in a constant state of excitement.

There was a special way of keeping track of time. Harry

Good, the linguist, didn't have much on his plate at this stage so he was given the time keeping task. He used the Earth calendar and every 24 hours marked off a day. This system worked out fine. They floated along with no sensation of speed because there were no visible objects to measure it by; just space and more space. Oh yes, there were spheres out in space but they were so far away it took days or even months to see any change in position. It was repeated many times over, "What a wonderful experience"!!!

The weeks flipped by and then the months. The crew played cards, read books, listened to music, and carried on many hours of conversation speculating what they would find in the days ahead. Time passed without seemingly a dull moment. They were a happy bunch. Betty Simms kept the place neat and tidy. She gave orders too, "Who left their slippers lying in the middle of the living room"? Or, "How many times do I have to tell you to put your laundry in the laundry basket"? She meant it but said it in such a way that nobody took offence to it.

After 7 months of travel some changes did start to show. A slice of Earth was now hidden by the sun and this would increase as they moved further around their orbit. All members were now peering ahead to see if they could see any evidence of the sought after planet. One day Fred Wong, one of the techs, called out, "Come and look". They rushed to the window and with sun glasses on, peered at the sun. Sure enough there was a tiny slit of a large sphere showing. As they moved on it would become larger. There was great celebration in Moonbeam that day. Jim Bolder came out of the galley and said, "Are you sure that is not Earth and we are on our way home"? There was a roar of laughter and Toni Jaski screamed out, "Get back in the kitchen and don't even suggest such a thing".

As they moved on they could see it quite clearly and Sally started doing some calculations. She concluded that it must be at least the same size as Earth. Speculation began on whether it was inhabited or if it had a compatible atmosphere. Would they be able to land on it? Of course they had space suits that would allow them to leave the ship, at least for a short time.

It was another month before they could see the whole sphere of their new planet. They just needed to get closer in before they could determine much more about it. As they were cruising along Captain Bill thought he saw a flash of light in the distance. He alerted the crew and they all peered out of the windows and then the ship's instruments indicated that there was another object within their space. It turned out to be a strange space vehicle similar to those UFO's as seen on Earth. It followed them for three days and then started moving up on them. Sally sent out radio signals but there was no response. Surely if they were hostile they would have shown some sign of it. Gradually the craft moved up and positioned itself off the port side of Moonbeam. Bill rocked Moonbeam back and forth in a friendly gesture and the UFO responded in a like manner and then sped off in another direction.

The crew did not see anything of this spacecraft for another month. As they neared their new found planet they could start to make out some of its features. They thought they could make out oceans and land masses. Some parts seemed to be shrouded in clouds. In their excited discussions they reasoned that the new planet may have the same atmosphere as Earth and they would be able to leave Moonbeam without their space suits. Could they be that lucky? They decided to orbit the planet a couple of times before approaching for a landing. As they slowed and started a gradual descent Bill noticed that they the once again had company. This time the spacecraft seemed to be beckoning them to follow and perhaps lead them to a suitable place to land. As it turned out this was certainly the case. They were now into the atmosphere of the planet and Dr. Roberts cautioned the crew that they must follow the drill instructions before opening the door.

As they approached a flat grassy area the guide ship circled around indicating that they could land here. Moonbeam made an almost vertical descent and with retro-jets turned on, came down with a gentle thump. The techs took in specimens of air through a special tube and did their tests. This took some time but they came to the conclusion that it would support human life. There were some minor differences but it appeared to be non-toxic. The temperature outside was 18 degrees Celsius. Fred Wong volunteered to take the first breath. There was a special cell on the ship that was big enough to hold one person and also be isolated from the main body of the ship. Fred crawled in and the door was sealed behind him. He allowed some air to enter the compartment and then very cautiously took a small sniff. With no apparent discomfort he started to breathe normally. Fred notified the others through the intercom that the air had slight sweet smell to it but otherwise was no different from the air on Earth.

This was the signal to open the main door and the crew filed out. They all hugged one another and were glad to be on solid land again. By this time their friendly guide had landed not far away. The crew was approaching them. They were tall, bronze skinned, very similar to them, male and female, and they looked curious but friendly. Bill waved to them and they responded in a like manner. As they came up to our ship the apparent leader spoke the first word. He pointed to the ground and said, "Dooma", and then pointed to himself and said, "Groota". Bill pointed to himself and said, "BILL". They all laughed and offered hands for a hearty handshake. As they talked among themselves Harry Good saw that he had a big job ahead of himself. He was the linguist and would have to figure out how to communicate with these people who he decided to call Doomans.

After a few indiscernible introductions the Doomans took their leave and headed for some nearby buildings. The crew decided to stay with their ship until they managed a few more words of communication. It was all so strange and yet wonderful. Their theory about a second earthlike planet had certainly proved to be true. Their plan was to stay here and explore the place before returning to Earth, maybe even a year hence. Knowing that they had lost communication with Earth it may give them a certain feeling of isolation.

The sun was setting, bringing an end to an historic and happy day for our travelers. The rotation of Dooma was a bit slower than Earth making their days an hour longer and also Dooma was a little bit larger than Earth adding another hour to the day. They had to adjust to a 26 hour day so that they had to change their whole time system from days through weeks and months to years. This seemed to be simpler for them than trying to change seconds in a minute and minutes in an hour because their clocks were already set and couldn't be changed. Another thing they had to adjust to was their weight. Because the force of gravity was stronger everything was proportionally heavier. This was fact they just had to get used to.

Chapter Three

After a good nights sleep the crew rose to a hearty breakfast prepared by their expert cook. After the beds were made up and the place was tidied up Bill called a meeting of the crew. The first task would be to get Harry Good working with some of the Doomans to try and work out lingual communication. This would have to be fairly advanced before they could hope to do much in the way of finding out how people lived on this planet. They wanted to mingle with the people in order to get a grasp of what society was like, how they made a living, and much, much more.

It was not long before a group of Doomans approached Moonbeam and, with a hand wave made it clear that it was a friendly visit. The leader, the same one that met them the day before, indicated that he wanted to communicate. Harry stepped forward and invited this man to join him at a table. An hour later great progress seemed to be taking place. They were using sign language and uttering single syllable words and every now and then laughing aloud. They were having a wonderful time.

Meanwhile the rest of the crew was showing the others around their ship and doing quite a lot of sign language as well. It became clear that the Doomans wanted the crew to accompany them to the nearby city. Harry had discovered that they were invited to lunch. Now this could be interesting. They had no idea what would be served for lunch. It was clear that there were cultivated gardens nearby and Harry had found out that they cooked their food on stoves. Beyond that it was a mystery. Groota took an instrument from his pocket and communicated with someone somewhere. It became evident very quickly who he had called because a bus drove up and they were invited aboard. As they moved away there was just a very slight hum to the motor or whatever was propelling them along. There was certainly no visible smoke or odor from it. It would be some time before things like this could be divulged because of the language difference.

The bus came to a halt in front of a long building that turned out to be a large mess hall. The building appeared to be made of a plastic material. The windows were made of a glass-like material. The long dining table was lined with comfortable chairs and cutlery and dishes were very similar to those on Earth. Before seating the Doomans, standing behind their chairs, broke into a sort of chant. It was quite musical and easy to listen to. It must be some form of religious routine. When it was finished Groota motioned to his guests to be seated. Beautiful young Dooman girls brought in steaming hot vegetables and some other dishes of fish. It was a very tasty meal capped off with a desert of fresh fruit, not unlike what the Earthlings ate back home. It would take some getting used to a little difference in taste but it certainly was not distasteful.

After dinner the crew was treated to a short dance performance by a group of colorfully young people. A young man came out and sang a song. The lyrics were Dooman but music is universal and our crew gave them a good round of applause.

The entertainment being over, the crew was invited into another building with offices with men and women working at desks. They had what looked like computers and other office machines. There was a reception and the crew was asked to sign a visitors' book. They were the first Earthlings in the book. All this was very thrilling for them and they declared that this was going to be a wonderful experience—too easy to be true.

They returned to the bus and were taken back to Moonbeam where they relaxed for the rest of the day. Sally Post noted that the Doomans used the written word and marveled at the modern offices. Betty Simms wondered how they could get in touch with Earth. Could it be that she was a bit homesick? She insisted that she wasn't but was thinking about what the people back home were doing and were they worrying about the fate of the crew.

The next few days were used up by Language study. The crew so badly wanted to be able to communicate with their newfound friends. They wanted to visit their homes and schools and learn as much about the culture as they could. Bill told them to calm down and relax. They had plenty of time and of utmost importance at the time was language. The Dooman language was very difficult to learn whereas the Doomans seemed to have little difficulty with English. English, by this time, had become almost universal on Earth so this is the language the Earthlings used here.

Something else they noticed that the bus ran on what looked like rubber tires but what propelled them remained a mystery. Time would tell. This is when the crew realized what a huge mission they were on. Everything had to be recorded. Each crew member carried a notebook and was constantly writing in them.

Harry was starting to pick up some of the Dooman language which proved to be very helpful. He learned that one of the top scientists wanted to meet them and share some of their knowledge. Arrangements were made for the crew to take a tour of one of the huge laboratories. The next morning the bus arrived and off they went. As they pulled into the front gate of the establishment they noted that there were only about ten cars parked in the small parking lot. They were ushered into the building only to find hundreds of people working there. How did they get to and from work? The city was ten miles away and it is very unlikely that they walked. The explanation was simple. Each home had a stairwell or elevator that led down to long platforms where the people boarded fast moving trains. They ran almost silently, taking the people back and forth to work. The Doomans had found a way to harness magnetism thus doing away with pollution. They were all underground and only required minimal ventilation. It was a very efficient way of transporting large numbers of people. It was also discovered that all their vehicles used the same source of energy.

As it turned out the crew met with five eminent scientists and despite a bit of difficulty with the language they were able to learn a great deal about Dooman technology. Betty was particularly curious about radio communication because she was anxious to contact Earth. They told her that they were able to contact their space craft when orbiting Earth. They had established communication stations on other planets and could bounce signals wherever they wanted to. Betty asked if it would be possible to use their system to try to contact Earth to which they agreed. There were stations on Earth constantly scanning for radio signals from outer space and perhaps they could pick up a signal from her. Plans would be made to set up the equipment on the following day.

The head of the scientific group was a tall handsome man by the name of Gort. He was an electronics specialist and he headed up a large team of people researching in that field. As an example of one result of their research they had developed a system that supplied all their power needs from the sun. Along with magnetic power, it ran their trains, buses, cars, and supplied all the power to run their lighting system and power their office equipment. Factories were run entirely on power from the sun. It was thus that Dooma had little or no significant pollution caused by people.

For air transportation the Doomans used craft similar to the UFO's seen on Earth. They did not require the huge airports like those on Earth. Their craft made vertical take off and landings and only required landing pads similar to Earth's helipads. Thus passengers and freight could be picked up or delivered almost anywhere without the massive congestion seen at Earth's airports.

Toni Jaski, one of the techs, asked them about the material that all the buildings were made of. That was another marvelous bit of technology. They harvested trees from specific areas of forest, areas that could easily be re-forested. The whole trees were hauled to the factory where they were fed into huge shredding machines. The resulting mash was carried by conveyer belts into large vats where other materials, including water, sand, cement, fine stone, and coloring was added and mixed into an emulsion. It was then poured off into specifically shaped moulds. These moulds were then moved forward into large ovens and the material was allowed to set into fireproof shapes to form parts of buildings. A whole house could be poured in a day. The moulds were constructed in an adjoining part of the factory. Plans were designed and drawn up by engineers and fed into a computer. The operator could just press a button and equipment put the mould together in a matter of minutes. Another push of a button makes the selection and the appropriate mould moves out for use.

This was indeed a very informative day for the crew of Moonbeam. While they were visiting the lab Gort asked them if they would like to have a house put up near their ship and then they wouldn't have to be cooped up in crowded quarters. It would be erected and ready to move into in two days. When they asked how they could pay for it Gort shrugged his shoulders and didn't understand what they meant. With some difficulty because of language it was explained to them that there was no monetary system on Dooma. Commodities, including food and clothing, were supplied as required. The Doomans had done away with the monetary system several centuries ago. "This is incredible", retorted Bill. Gort explained that their people had been taught from childhood that trust and honesty were virtues to be upheld throughout life. People had learned that working was a right and an obligation in order to be recognized Doomans. They were fanatically proud of their being and seemed to be living a very carefree life.

Two days later the crew has a brand new house, fully furnished Dooman style with a fully modern kitchen and comfortable furniture. The house had been brought up in large sections, set in place and bolted together with special fasteners. When the structure was completed the furnishing were brought up and installed in a matter of hours. There was no muss or clutter. Everything was clean and tidy, ready to go. Now the crew had plenty of room for their quarters and they could use the ship as a research base. June and Mary were thrilled with the new kitchen with all its new gadgets. By now the crew was getting used to Dooman food and they could conserve their own food stocks in Moonbeam for the journeys ahead.

Chapter Four

Early one morning there was a rap on the door and a young man asked, with some difficulty, if Betty Simm could come to the laboratory with him. Apparently Gort wanted to see if they could communicate with Earth. She and Bill got into the vehicle and off they went to the lab. The lad led them into a room full of "electronic" equipment and they were greeted by Gort. He actually greeted Betty and Bill with a hearty, "Good morning". Evidently Harry's lessons were paying off. Gort indicated that the equipment was all hers. It was quite easy to figure out. Gort had already set the equipment to contact a spaceship in Earth's orbit. Now all that was necessary was to send a blanket signal into the same area. It was a universal signal used for research purposes. Betty pressed the button to send out the signal and waited for a response. In a few moments there was a crackling sound and a few whistles and then the waited for code. They had made contact. Now she wanted to make voice contact. After a good deal of dial adjustments there came a voice of complete amazement. They were hearing a voice in Earth language and they realized they had reached contact with Moonbeam. They exchanged heartfelt greetings and Betty described their position and informed this person whom she knew as Gordon that they would be staying on their research project for some time – probably about a year. There was great jubilation back at Moonbeam that night. Arrangements would soon be made to contact relatives and friends back home. The crew would be able to consult with the technical support staff at home base on Earth.

Gort was making arrangements to have a station set up in Moonbeam so that they could communicate as often as they wanted to. All this was like a fairy tale coming true. This was a time to crack a bottle of Dooman wine. Yes, they had kept the habit of making and enjoying wine. Other alcoholic beverages had not been seen by the crew to this time. The Doomans were lovers of social gatherings and their form of sports events. They had various types of musical instruments. They were great dancers and loved to sing. In all their performances there was no violence. To sum it all up the Doomans were lovers of peace and happiness. The rare appearance of policemen seemed to be devoted to directing traffic or overseeing sports events. They were noted for their athletic stature and ability.

There were super highways connecting cities and towns. All vehicles were equipped with electronic devices that automatically prevented accidents. When one vehicle got too close to another one, they automatically repulsed each other. Sensors controlled speed according to road or temperature conditions. All this may sound too good to be true but it must be remembered that they were a thousand years ahead of the people on Earth.

We are soon to find out how all this was accomplished. It all seemed to be centered around home and family. There was no competition over wealth and money, and most particularly competition over power. Through proper distribution there was plenty for all. It all started from the time a child was born and was a major point of research for our crew from Earth. They had to get invited into the home to see how the children were raised. The Doomans were only too willing to have Earthling come and stay for awhile. They too were very keen to learn about their visitors from so far away. Jane Silver was the first to go in to a home in the city. She soon discovered a big difference in the way children were treated.

In the first place they were nurtured by very devoted and loving parents. There was need for only one parent to work so there was always one of them at home. Both could have jobs but not at the same time. Only one of them could be away from the children in a twenty six hour period. Babies were breast fed for the first eight months. There was no sticking a bottle in the baby's mouth and rushing off to work leaving the baby with a sitter. Mother was restricted from working for the first year. Her time was totally devoted to the child.

When a couple married it was mandatory that they both take a parenting course. Children were brought up to be proud Doomans, to respect their elders, to love their parents and siblings, and to generally get along with others. They were spared the blast of loud music and violence via the media. There were no video parlors to introduce them to gun violence and road racing. Their alternative was a reasonable sound level to all programmed material, interesting stories on TV without serious violence. There were no video parlors, no toys that were replicas of war weapons. They had Disney like movies and plenty of other movies of interest for all ages. The children were happy and engaged in many games both indoors and outdoors. Discipline was fair and not violent; much like the animals of the forest disciplines their young.

This may seem like a socialist way of life but it had become a universal way of raising children. When they went to school they were treated in the same manner as at home. Their main aim in life was to enjoy living and become good Doomans. When the Doomans saw that there had to be a huge change in the way they lived they adopted this method and it had worked very well for the past five hundred years. Of course there were growing pains. Wars and all weapons of war had to be removed. Huge museums were built where the relics of war were kept as a grim reminder of the past. All records were kept here as well and our Earth crew was invited here only to see an almost replica of what was now in use on Earth. Could the people on Earth adopt this as a new way of life?   Dooma was successful in making the transformation. Why couldn't the people of Earth do the same? It is for certain that changing religious beliefs would be the most difficult challenge.   Changing the educational system and the raising of children would become a close second.

These were the conclusions that the members of the crew came to after they had gone over the reports each one made on return from their host families. The Doomans had mastered a very good method of raising their children and it carried on into adulthood. The children were not abused in any way. They knew from the very beginning that mother and father were the authority and like bear cubs in the forest they obeyed orders.

The outstanding question was how the Doomans managed the big change from the time when they were in the same situation politically as Earth was at that time. The first thing they had to do was to find a way of running the whole community of the planet without the use of politicians. This was a huge step and not an easy one. A global council was set up with representatives from each country. These people took extensive training in economic affairs. All of the officials, two from each country, took the same training and were responsible for applying what they learned in their own respective countries. It must be remembered that all the countries on Dooma had to agree that drastic measures had to be taken in order to save the planet. Each city had a city hall and a mayor. He was actually a go-between for the people and the council. It took a couple of decades to smooth out the big bumps in this system but amazingly enough it worked. The combination of the council training program and the education program for children all grew into the system and were happy to see a solution to war and disorder. The people themselves had the responsibility of making it work. All war materials, weapons, and war machines were immediately done away with. Samples were paced in a very large museum and could only be viewed by historians and those who needed a reminder of the horrors of human conflict.

There were tanks, guns, warships, fighter aircraft, and thousands of books telling the history of past wars. There were also relics of civil crime and stories about the futility of trying to control by armed force.

Chapter Five

Now the crew was ready for the next research project which was to go further afield and see other parts of the planet. Gort suggested that the crew board one of their craft and two of them come along to help out with language and introductions, etc. It was decided that he and Groota would join them and then of course their flight crew would be included. Preparations would be made and they would leave the next morning. Where would they go? Bill and Sally had pored over maps supplied by their hosts and they decided that a tropical area would prove interesting. There was a large island about 1,000 miles south of the equator. This would be a good start.

With all their gear on board they climbed on board this strange space vehicle. It was very spacious and comfortable. They required no more than common seat belts for the take-off. As they sped off there was just a very faint hum. On board they enjoyed a Dooman flight breakfast and in a couple of Dooman hours were descending for a landing. They all exited the ship to a hot sunny day. It was a bit humid and there was a pleasant breeze blowing off the water. They were met by a welcoming group of five Doomans. Their skin was darker than their northern neighbors but they spoke the same language and wore wide smiles on their faces. The women were very good looking and dressed in scant clothing to suit the climate. The men wore what looked like short skirts and many wore no upper garments.

Introductions were exchanged and all were ushered into an open building with a grass thatched roof. Harry and Groota acted as interpreters and a serious conversation ensued. Each member of the Earth crew had a specific area of interest to explore. Arrangements were made for each one of them to be accompanied by local members to help them in their quest.

There was a hospital nearby and Dr. Tom Morgan indicated that he would like to go there and see the facility. Jane Silver wanted to go along to have a look at the hospital housekeeping, laundry, and other aspects of sanitation. Mary Swan joined them to look at food distribution and the dietary needs of patients. The group was met at the hospital by the head of medicine and two nurses. The nurses were very striking in their white uniforms trimmed with green.

The group was led into a reception office where they were briefed on patient care and also the common causes for the need for hospital care. The Doomans had long since found a cure for many of the common ailments found on Earth such as cancer, leukemia, tuberculosis, and many of the common children diseases. It was mentioned earlier that on arrival the Earthlings had noticed a sweet smell in the air. It was explained that the Doomans had developed a system that would continuously spray a mild antiseptic into the atmosphere. There were tall silos scattered around the country to house this equipment.

As they were shown through the wards it was noted that most of the patients were there for treatment of injuries resulting from industrial or sports activities. There was a children's ward to treat bumps and bruises nut very few cases of common diseases. It was remarkable to the visitors from Earth. Finally they were shown into the ward for the aged. Here also were cases of broken bones and other injuries caused from falls and the like. It was explained by the head surgeon that in all of Dooma it was a common occurrence to practice euthanasia. If, at the age of eighty, or even before, a person felt that he/she had no more purpose to life a request could be made

to end their life. In Dooman culture it was considered to be an heroic act. Of course it was not done without ample consultation with the patient and the family. It may sound a bit morbid to the reader but after generations of this practice it became commonplace and generally accepted. All bodies were cremated and placed in niches in columbiums with respect and honor. Subsequently there was less need for extended care facilities and old age homes. Natural deaths were treated in the same manner freeing up large areas formerly used for cemeteries.

For the normal illnesses medications were prescribed by the doctors most of which were derived from plants. Each store had a small drug corner and of course these drugs were available with a note from the doctor. There were medical centers where minor injuries could be attended to with out appointments. It might be added that doctors made house calls day or night.

In the meantime Fred Wong and Toni Jaski, the two techs made good use of their time exploring the Dooman spacecraft. The crew of the ship, one of who had attended Harry's language lessons, was only too pleased to show off their marvelous craft. It too operated on converted energy from the sun. It was capable of traveling to all parts of the solar system as well as serve as an airline for local use. It too was capable of vertical landings and take-offs. It had retractable landing gear that could be used for taxiing once on the ground. When asked about "crop circles" left on Earth they said that these were spots where they had actually landed on Earth hoping to attract attention. They wanted to make contact with earthlings but were uncertain of the welcome they would get. With their new communications setup they were planning to make contact electronically and now that they had some Earth language it should be quite simple. Toni explained to them that the situation on Earth was not very good. She said that Dooma was a perfect example to follow and that as soon as they returned to Earth they would make every effort to publicize life on Dooma and perhaps influence some changes to work toward the Dooma way of life. They explained to her that the greatest stumbling blocks would be religion and greed. Once that is overcome, the rest will be relatively easy.

As evening was approaching both crews were invited into a large dining hall. After a scrumptious meal they were entertained by some young dancers and beautiful soothing music similar to Hawaiian music. Next to the dining hall was another building resembling an hotel. The guests are shown to very comfortable bedrooms where they would sleep during their visit. There was no question of paying for anything. There was no money.

After a hearty breakfast the earthlings were invited to visit some farms and factories. They would see first hand how food was grown and how it was processed. There were large fields of different types of grain and vegetables. There were also large orchards that produce many varieties of fruit. All plant-life was luscious with no sign of damage from insects or plant diseases. The Dooman produce, although similar to that produced on Earth, was different. The fruit was large and very juicy – delicious. They saw large farm vehicles hauling the produce to large buildings where it was prepared for delivery to stores. These food processing plants were fully automated and could turn out tons of product every hour of the day. The workers appeared to be happy and contented at their jobs. They worked for four Dooman hours and then were relieved by another shift.

There was also a fishing industry including fish boats and a fish processing plant. The fishermen went out to sea much the same as fishermen on Earth. A large quantity of fish was frozen for immediate shipment and a large quantity was canned. To the earthlings it seemed uncanny that these people followed the same procedures as was done back home. Even their counters and food processing machines were made of what appeared to be stainless steel. Everything was spotless clean. Sanitation was a top priority.

This tropical island produced an enormous amount of agricultural product and was still a super vacation spot. The hospitality was beyond comparison. The crews boarded the ship with a sense of reluctance and many of the residents came to see them off. With an almost silent take-off they were on their way. Bill decided that they should return to their camp in order to get all their paper work done – computer work.

Chapter Six

Back at their Dooman home the crew got to work documenting what they had experienced on the island. They had taken many pictures on video and they burned them onto discs to make up hours of documentaries. With the help of Grooten, Betty was able to send some pictures back to Earth along with some description of life on the newfound planet. Most important of all, of course, was the welfare of the members of the expedition.

Apart from their work, Grooten and Betty seemed to be a little more than enjoying their work together. Bill noticed this and decided to keep an eye on them. Betty was a beautiful lady and Grooten, as mentioned before, was a tall handsome man. They were about the same age and made a fine looking couple. Could a romance be budding?

The next excursion would be to the Dooman North where they would certainly encounter cold winter conditions. By description this part of the country was inhabited by Doomans similar to Earth's Finns or even Canada's Eskimos. It was decided that all members of the Moonbeam crew would take the trip in their own ship. The day before departure a couple of Doomans came up with warm clothing and tents suitable for northern climate. Once again Grooten offered his services as a guide and interpreter. Bill agreed and he noticed that Betty was very pleased with his decision.

The next morning, well prepared, they boarded Moon-beam and were on their way. Sally Post set the course for due north and as they progressed they started to see snow. Very soon the outside thermometer registered – 40 degrees Celsius. Bill glided the ship down to an outcropping of ice next to a large expanse of water over which there was a light blanket of fog. Grooten

helped set up the camp. He was the head of a team of scientists that developed equipment for extreme cold conditions. The tents were double layered with a layer of insulation between the layers. When they were set up, Mary shouted out, "There is heat coming from this box". Grooten explained that he had worked with a group of scientists and they had developed a system that extracted heat from the sun and stored it for use in the heater. What luxury would they find next?

They were not here very long before a strange looking vehicle approached their camp. It appeared to be some sort of hover - craft. Four individuals alit and greeted the crew with the same enthusiasm as all other Doomans they had met. They were very curious about this strange looking space-craft. They had thought it was a supply ship bringing in supplies. When they saw the crew they were amazed at their appearance and were further amazed to learn that they were from another planet. Mary prepared a fine meal for all she was thrilled that the appliances supplied by the Doomans were self heating.

Their new found friends enjoyed Mary's meal and stayed on for an hour asking many questions about life on Earth. These people operated a scientific station two miles from there and they invited Bill to bring his crew for a visit. Bill said,

"We will be there tomorrow". With that they sped off in a swirl of snow. Our party got settled down for a good nights sleep in the tents.

The next morning they boarded Moonbeam and took a low-level flight to explore the area. They expected to see some wildlife but none were visible at this time. Bill brought the ship down at a small settlement. There were children playing in the snow and men shoveling fresh snow from paths between buildings. It was easy to distinguish the main science building.

There were antennas sticking up in the air, a wind speed indicator and weather vain. After a good hot mug of Dooman broth they went to see the station. It was full of instruments and they were scanning outer space for foreign signals. They also studied the waters of the ocean and took seismic readings of the ground because there had been a series of earth quakes [pardon me, Dooman quakes] in the area. There was no need to search for petroleum because they had already developed their new energy source.

For the next week they explored this northern tundra and they did spot some animals that looked much like polar bears and reindeer. They didn't see any seal like animals so assumed they didn't live here. However they did see a number of stations spotted along the coast. Bill pointed out some tall silo looking structures and decided to revisit the first camp and find out what they were for. It turned out these housed experimental equipment that they hoped would be able to harness energy from the aurora borealis [northern lights]. Groota went into a bit more detail, explaining that it had a lot to do with magnetic power but it was still in its early development.

They noted as well that there was an absence of that sweet smell in the air that was so noticeable back at their first landing site. They questioned Grooten about it and he told them that, due to the cold climate, it was not necessary. Fred Wong had managed to get some soil samples to take back and analyze. Satisfied with their excursion they headed back to home base.

When they got back there was a crew at their site working on what looked like another building. It turned out to be a shelter for Moonbeam. They feared that the hot sun may do some damage to the ship. They needn't have bothered because the ship was designed to withstand much higher temperatures while in outer space. So be it! A little more luxury won't hurt!

By this time the crew had been away for four months and at times felt a bit of homesickness, but as Bill explained there was still much of the planet they had not yet visited. Oh well, the life here was good and they could communicate with home whenever they wanted to. Betty certainly didn't seem to be in any hurry to leave. She and Grooten were certainly showing interest in one another. Bill and Dr. Tom Morgan decided to have a talk with her. Intimate relations may have a devastating result.

At the first opportunity Bill and Tom invited Betty to a private interview. Bill said to her'"We have notice that you and Grooten have been spending quite a bit of time together and we are wondering if there is something going on that we should know about". Betty's face reddened a bit and she replied, "Grooten is a very nice person to work with and together we have accomplished a lot in communication. We have been able to secure a link with Earth and are now working to expand our work into outer space. I know that Grooten thinks a great deal of me and in fact we have discussed the possibilities of a lasting relationship". Tom asked her if she had thought about the ramifications of the possibility of a union resulting in a child. She answered him squarely, "Yes, we have discussed it but feel that it is too early to make such serious decisions". "Well thank goodness for that because you understand that there would have to be an extensive genetic study done before undertaking such a union. You must understand that we are willing to work with Dooman doctors to carry on this research". To this suggestion Betty did not object and in fact seemed relieved that this meeting had taken place.

On the following morning Tom met with a couple of Dooman doctors who were working specifically with genetics. They told him that they were expecting the return of a crew from Mars in a couple of days. They were bringing soil samples back with them to see if they could find any evidence of DNA. In the meantime the clinic would get samples of Grooten's DNA and Tom would get a sample from Betty. They had no idea what they may discover and made arrangements to spend time in the lab when the Mars expedition arrived.

After the days work was done Grooten and Betty were seen walking together to a park seat some distance away. They looked to be in very deep and serious conversation. They stayed out there until well after sunset before returning to camp. There is no doubt what they were talking about. Of course all eyes were on them as Grooten gave Betty a "goodnight kiss"

After a few days Bill and Tom were sent for. They were greeted warmly by the research team and were ushered into the lab. They had established some amazing facts. They had indeed found DNA in the soil samples from Mars. More amazing was the fact that there were matching factors with Dooman DNA. Now they anxiously awaited the results of the couples DNA tests. Would there be enough similarity to al-

low a union to produce a child? There was vast talk and speculation in camp as the crew awaited the results of the tests.

Finally the results were announced and sure enough
such a union could produce a child. Betty was thrilled at the
news but said that she was not quite ready to make a final
decision. If they decided to become a couple would they have
a Dooman wedding or would Grooten return to Earth with
them and have an Earth wedding? Time would tell.

Now the big question presented itself, how did the DNA
get from one planet to another? The answer was under their
noses all the time. DNA particles were present in space dust
and could reach any body in the universe. Some could land
in certain places, probably tropical and in water and nature
took its course. As time was of no consequence natural evolution took place and all creatures evolved including man and
woman. The DNA could come to rest on any terrestrial body
but of course could only develop where conditions were favorable. There had to be water, atmosphere, and suitable climatic
conditions to support life. To satisfy the Theologians, it may
be suggested that the Lord waved his hand over the swamp
and mankind was born. All the rest can be fit into place.

From the earliest of times man has believed in a Godly power over the universe and has gone to all ends to worship their Gods. These beliefs were even evident on Dooma.
There was no evidence of the huge houses of worship found on
Earth. The Doomans did congregate on certain days and went
through some sort of religious activities. When Bill made inquiries about it he was told that at the time of the great change
the Doomans had adopted a single form of worship that ap-
plied to whatever God the people believed in. It took a couple
of centuries to iron out all the problems but at the present all
seemed to be working. Religious wars had been completely

eradicated. What a wonderful plan to be taken back to Earth!

Of course there was no celebration of Christmas on Dooma because Christianity was unheard of. However they did have a great feast day in the spring when they exchanged greetings and gifts. This festival lasted for three days. It seems that this is universally human nature. It may also be noted here that we have adopted the name human for all creatures in the form of man

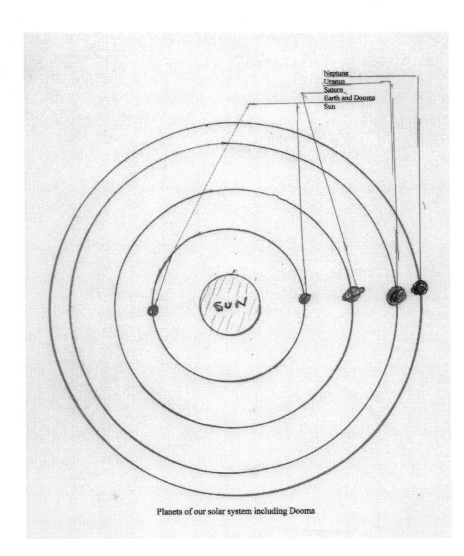

Neptune
Uranus
Saturn
Earth and Dooma
Sun

SUN

Planets of our solar system including Dooma

This picture shows the relative size of the planets in orbit around our sun and their relative distance from the sun. However it does not indicate at what position they are in as they travel around the sun. For the sake of our story the planet Dooma would be in the same orbit as Earth but on the other side of the sun. This is why it is not visible from Earth

Chapter Seven

The next journey for the crew would be to the other side of Dooma. Here they were told that they may be in for some surprises. The people here were of a different culture. The crew got Moonbeam loaded up and ready for another adventure. Once again Grooten was a member of the crew. It was pretty much understood now that Betty and Grooten was a couple. They did not share a bed nor did they intend to until if and when they decided to marry.

In the morning moonbeam made a graceful take-off and headed in an easterly direction. They were in the air for twelve hours before putting down in a pretty setting near the sea. The people who came to greet them were blacks. They had been forewarned of the visit so had made preparations for a great feast. The food was cooked over an open fire and served in the open air on a long banquet table. These people were very formal and gave a short bow when speaking to the strangers. Grooten acted as interpreter and a tall handsome man acted as host.

The guests were settled into a facility similar to the one they had stayed in on the island. The next   thing was to find out what the people did here. This part of Dooma was very rich in minerals so there were many mining operations. The crew was shown into a large building where several metals were separated from rock and melted down. The molten metals was then passed into large molds and formed into ingots.

The ingot passed into another building where the finer processing took place. The ingots were again melted and portions taken to be mixed with other metals to make alloys. For instance, if they wanted to make a certain tool they could make up the appropriate alloy and it was passed on to the tool makers. All procedures were computer controlled and the workers had merely to push buttons. All were very well educated and expert at what they were doing.

The women in this part of the planet did not work in the factories or in the mines. There was also a very large agricultural industry here and many of the women worked in the fields and in the processing plants. Those who had children stayed home. They took parenting very seriously which was reflected in the behavior of the children. Politeness was a major factor in their upbringing. Toni and Tom visited a couple of the schools and could easily see where the politeness and formality came from. Most of the basic skills of reading and writing had been taught at home. Computers were widely used in the schools and all the children were attentive and willing to learn. They were recognized as the next generation of technicians, doctors and community leaders. It was a pleasure to be among these children. Every one of them seemed to have a purpose and a pride in being a Dooman. There may have been the odd spitball fired across the classroom but if there was it was not observed by their visitors.

It may be wondered why very few black people were not seen in other parts of Dooma visited by the crew from Earth. Upon inquiry they were told that these people were perfectly happy where they were and saw no need to travel. Of course they sent delegates to global conferences and special meetings. They were certainly free to travel back and forth if they so desired. Many did travel because they took holidays as earthlings did and were seen in the many vacation areas. There was no discrimination either way.

There were two very large cattle ranches here. They were major suppliers of meat and dairy products for all the planet's needs. There was very little difference in appearance of the cows from those on Earth. The dairy barns were kept spotless clean and all dairy products were processed on site. Milk was piped into the city to a large dispensing facility where the people could come and get milk as needed. Other dairy products were available as well.

Bill decided to stay here for awhile longer because these people were so very kind to them and besides the people there wanted to learn much more about planet Earth. They spent much of their time at the dairies and with Grooten's help with the language they learned how the Doomans cared for their animals with respect to diet and disease control. All their animals were clean and healthy. When they visited the slaughter house and meat packing plant Jim Bolder became very interested in how the meat was handled. The Doomans had many meat products that the chef had never seen before. He was kept busy taking notes and looking forward to the day he could use some of the recipes. There didn't seem to be any bosses around keeping track of the workers. They just came to work and did what they were supposed to do. There was an office staff of girls and their job was to keep track of inventory a look after shipping of orders.

Finally the crew was satisfied with what they discovered and was ready to take their leave. There was another big farewell feast of steaks, fruit, and fresh vegetables. They took some of the odd looking fruit back with them. It was delicious. In the morning they were off home to their base.

There was no sign of political wrangling in this land and Bill was determined to see what he could find out about it. Grooten took them to an office where all could be explained. Apparently the Doomans had gone through a long period of political disorder and when the big change came about the Dommans world council had opted to a new order that excluded politicians on a local level. All major planning came from the world council and was handed down to committees in each country. There was a mayor of each city and it was up to him and his staff to relay any changes to the educators. So it was that the rules of the land were taught in the schools and universities. Straying from this system meant immediate dismissal from that position of authority. The two representatives from each country were chosen by the people to attend world council meetings and this is where all major decisions were made. Amazingly it worked very well because all the people knew what was going on. The needs of a particular part of the country were passed up to the world council and were dealt with there. So it was determined that the solution came down to education. It worked.

All this means is that behavior is a learned process. This is how people learn to talk, to walk, to play, and all the other things that make us what we are. Unfortunately those bad traits are also taught, all with good intentions. Starting with the new born; we expose the little one to very loud noise in the form of modern music, perhaps smoke or other forms of foul air. We can't wait to give them toys that suggest violence and prime it with violence via the television and later via the computer. The video parlors are perhaps the worst and then we expect our children to live a peaceful, law-abiding life.

The Doomans saw this and the need for change. Staring in the home, through parent education, they were able to get the children off to a good start. On into the schools the process continued and all violent and abusive material was removed from the media and the video parlors. It had to be done with no exceptions in order to make their plan work and have a peaceful planet. Now the crew from Earth could make the comparison between the ways of life on each planet. Life can be a wonderful experience for all of the people, not just for a select few. It is said that money is the root of all evil, the mentor of greed. Well, the Doomans did away with the use of money and relied upon the good nature of their people to supply the needs of their world. Their reward was the good life, free from strife and conflict, free from fear of their neighbors. They had a life built on trust backed by the pride of being Doomans. They had viewed the situation on Earth and exalted in the fact that they had lived through a similar era and had successfully managed to put it right. Their efforts were now able to concentrate on the good things of life rather than trying to develop better means of destroying one another. The question that clouded the members of the crew from Earth was how they could ever hope to convey this to the people on Earth when they returned. The Doomans were only too pleased to talk about their great transformation of a thousand years before. They knew that it had survived the test of time and would see to it that nothing changed.

Chapter Eight

Now it was time to do some serious homework and con-
solidate their findings into presentable reports so that if and
when they could contact Earth they could give accurate information. The first concern was, of course, was to let the people
back home know that they were safe and that they had landed
safely on the new-found planet.

The next morning Gort arrived in a fully equipped communications vehicle. He and Betty got right to work setting
up to send out signals to Earth. The plan was to use their station on Mars to bounce the signal toward Earth. Betty suggested that they use Earth's universal signal so that it would be
readily recognized by researchers on Earth. They programmed
the equipment to keep repeating the signal until they got a
response. In the meantime Gort kept scanning space for a
signal from Earth.

After many hours of trying Gort suddenly announced
that he thought he heard a response. Betty sent out an electronic voice message, "Moonbeam calling". This she kept
sending but got only a very faint beeping that didn't make any
sense. Then she sent out a message giving the Dooman co-
ordinate on Mars. A couple of hours later a louder message
came in, "Come in Moonbeam". They had made a positive

connection and could now exchange computerized messages both ways. This was a wonderful break-through and the crew could actually talk to their loved ones back home.

Gort offered to set up a station on site for them and they could use it all the time they were there. In a couple of days a small building was set up and fully equipped with a Dooman communications system. When Grooten came to visit Betty he was thrilled to see what had been accomplished. He had learned enough English that he would be able to send the first Dooman spoken message to Earth. This was indeed history in the making.

For the next two months the crew remained at their base location and continued to work on their reports and to mix with the Dooman families to thoroughly understand the way they lived. Harmony was the best way to express it. There was no quarrelling or arguing. If one disagreed with another's idea they seemed to be able to discuss it and come to a reasonable solution. The strongest feature of their lives seemed to be their pride in being Doomans. Going to work was natural to them and they took great pride in what they did.

The romance between Betty and Grooten continues to flourish. He called on her and they took in entertainment events together. They also attended counseling sessions and often Bill went along because, after all, he was responsible for her welfare. It was not yet decided if she would remain in Dooma or he would return to Earth with her. One thing was certain and that was that they wanted to marry and have children. Betty wanted her children to be raised Dooma style.

The Moonbeam crew had now been on the planet Dooma for over six months and winter was approaching. They were told to expect snow and cold weather. The Doomans provided them with winter clothing and assured them that their house would be warm and cozy. They were also provided them with two winter vehicles to travel around in. It seemed very strange that these vehicles glided along with very little noise and of course no pollution.

Harry Good continued to give lessons to the rest of the crew in the Dooman language so that now all of them could manage to get along in the community. With transportation they could travel to other communities where they got the same cordial reception. Of course there had been plenty of publicity about the visitors from Earth.

The crew often went out for an evening of entertainment. Most of the larger restaurants featured a live show every evening. Their music was quite a bit different because they had different instruments, many of them made of wood or a special plastic material. They had story tellers that told a wide variety of stories, in their own language of course. They were invited out to a dinner party one night where the Doomans presented a program in English in honor of the people from Earth. It seemed very strange not having to pay for anything. The entertainers would accept perhaps a bouquet of flowers but most of all they appreciated applause from their guests.

To this time it was noticed that the Doomans did not have white bread as that made on Earth. They ground up some sort of cereal grain whole and that was their flour. The grain was very similar to wheat and it is certain that it could probably be refined into white flour. Jim and Sally had a good idea how it was done and they were determined to teach the Doomans how to mill their grain and produce white flour. Here was a task for Betty. She was to communicate with Earth and get detailed instructions on the operation of a flour mill. The Doomans would quickly put it all together and voila; they had white bread. The possibilities were limitless. Through the communication system ideas could be exchanged very quickly. This served to bring a bit of home to the Earthlings and perhaps ward off some of the short spells of homesickness they sometimes had. Strangely enough it was Betty who seemed to yearn for home more than the others. Perhaps it was because she was so much looking forward to taking her Dooman husband back home.

The girls took the greatest enjoyment out of going to the shops and seeing all the Dooman ladies styles of clothing and accessories. Of course they could try them on and just check items out of the store as they wanted. Everything was displayed very nicely without price tags or sale signs. The clerks were only too pleased to help them with their selections and to explain the differences in quality. The girls were quite limited in what they could take because of the limited space in Moonbeam. Yes, the Dooman ladies used makeup and went to the beauty parlors to get their hair done. After all they had the same desire to attract the men as is done on Earth. Needless to say the men were very particular about their appearance as well. Courtship is indeed universal.

As the autumn approached the foliage on the trees and shrubs started changing into fall colors. The evenings were getting much cooler and the snow would be here about a month hence. One morning Bill queried, "I wonder if these people have a Christmas". Betty replied, "It seems like Christmas all year around here. Maybe this is paradise". They had learned that the Doomans did believe in a greater power and, as mentioned before, did have a short chant before meals. They also had special meetings where they chanted and had speakers but there were no great cathedrals or churches as on Earth. There were no signs of harsh language being spoken and voices were only raised when communicating at a distance, such as calling the children in for lunch. The children had playgrounds and equipment for climbing, sliding, and swinging, etc. There were swimming pools and special fields for ball sports. All their sports were supervised and were non-violent in nature. The children enjoyed themselves and of course injuries were rare. To say that these children were brain-washed would be far from the truth. They were not exposed to violence and therefore did not miss it. This sense of security and peacefulness carried on through their lives.

The Dooman houses and other buildings were heated from a central heating center. The heat was delivered by underground pipes to all the buildings. Temperatures could be regulated by thermostats in each building. This air was also purified from all forms of dust and pollutants. There were no furnaces to upkeep and of course complete freedom from chimney fires. All lighting in the homes was from solar light generation plants situated throughout the country. In some cases factories could produce some of their own electric power in the disposal of waste product; i.e. waste wood was burned and used to boil water to produce steam that was used to drive generators to produce electricity. This same technology had also been developed on Earth many years before.

The Doomans had almost completely done away with pollution in all areas. They were very conscientious about keeping their lakes and streams clean and healthy. The environment for wildlife was protected as well. Vast areas of parkland was set aside for animals and birds use. The only menace to the forest was fire and the Doomans had developed very efficient fire fighting equipment to help control this. They had no control over lightning but were working on developing water reservoirs in strategic places so that it was readily available for the fire fighters.

It was a pleasure to drive into a city without seeing that bank of smog and always be able to breathe that sweet fresh air. Dr. Tom Morgan said, "No wonder these people look so healthy. I'll bet you would be hard pressed to find anybody here suffering from asthma". Jane Silver joined in with, "Now you guys see why I am so fussy about keeping our quarters free of dust and dirt". They all had a good laugh but agreed that it was a good job they had such an efficient housekeeper in their crew. Dr. Tom had developed a sterilization routine to go through before returning to Earth but has since decided that it would not be necessary after living here this long,

One morning in mid October the crew woke up to see snow falling. The ground was covered and the whole area was a scene of beauty. Groota came up and invited Betty out for a bit of a game in the snow. He brought with him a toboggan like sled and they had a great time sliding down a nearby hill. The others were keen to join in and before nightfall there were enough sleds for everybody. Some of the children came up to join in on the fun. The day ended up with a camp fire and some good Gooman hot drinks. Sally brought out a feast of goodies she had prepared as the others played. This was exactly how they wanted to mix with the community and find out how the people lived.

As the winter progressed members of the crew were invited to Dooman schools to tell students about planet Earth. Of course they were not to talk about such things as war, crime, and corruption. They told the students about such things as the geography of Earth and about plant and animal life and how far Earth had progressed in the field of science. The latest developments in the field of space travel. This was a bit time consuming because they had to work with interpreters. The students were very keen to learn all they could about how people lived, what the schools were like, and what sports the kids played on Earth. It would not be hard to imagine how Earth children would react if an alien from outer space came to visit in their school. In any case the crew of Moonbeam thoroughly enjoyed this phase of their research.

Many of the boys and girls were intensely interested in studying science and particularly in becoming astronauts and exploring the universe. They were invited to come and see Moonbeam. They would see how far ahead the Doomans were in their space technology. Perhaps some of these scholars would eventually travel to Earth and help scientists there to catch up. Now that communication between the two planets had been established it was quite possible to transfer information back and forth. It was also realized that Earth would have to have its great time of change before there was much interchange between the two planets. It would be tragic to re-contaminate the Doomans with global conflicts now existing on Earth. It must be understood that only the top Dooman historians had knowledge of the terrible state their planet had experienced before their big change.

As mentioned earlier the Dooman girls were very attractive and they weren't backward about showing it. They had all the glamour of the Earth girls. As a matter of fact one very pretty lady seemed to be paying a lot attention to Captain Bill. He didn't exactly avoid or ignore her but, being Bill, he did not encourage her. Her name was Rosi and she often accompanied him when they went out dinner or entertainment. Rosi was a very intelligent girl and certainly was the fun of the party. She had made sure to attend most of the language sessions and was quite fluent in English. Rosi was also a very good singer. Bill insisted that there was only room for one more passenger on Moonbeam and that was reserved for

Groota. Betty and he were making definite arrangements for spring wedding and they indicated that he would go back to Earth with them. Other girls also accompanied the crew for nights out on the town. During that winter there were quite a few house parties at the crew's place.

When the Christmas season came there were no signs of celebrations and that seemed very strange to all members of the crew. The girls made sure to decorate their house and also put up some lights on Moonbeam. There was a large bird similar to a turkey that the Doomans cooked up for special occasions so Sally and Fred picked up one from the store and prepared it for Christmas Day. They invited some of their Dooman friends to come for Christmas dinner. There were also brightly wrapped gifts for all. They explained a bit about Earth religion but didn't try to push it on their guests. The evening was spent in feasting and music. The guests left about midnight to end a very delightful day.

Chapter Nine

Now as spring was approaching the crew of Moonbeam started thinking about their return trip to Earth. They had been away much longer than they had expected. They looked upon their adventure as being a complete success. They had seen and lived an ideal way of life. The Doomans had transformed their planet to a way of life that may be called paradise. The people from Earth now had a pattern to take home with them. What remained to be seen was how the Earth people would respond to the radical changes that needed to be made to recover the Earth from certain disaster. If the changes could be publicized sufficiently enough to convince the people to conform to these changes there was still hope for planet Earth.

Meanwhile Captain Williams had been working on plans to make some Dooman modifications to Moonbeam. Gort had introduced some very sophisticated upgrades to their communication system. They had installed a system that would repel space particles from the ship and thus avert possible damage to Moonbeam as they sped homeward. This would make future trips much safer and efficient. They would now be able to probe space at far greater distances than previously possible. Gort suggested that a team of Doomans were already planning a trip to Earth where they could meet again and now be assured a safe reception.

Betty and Groota were still making plans to marry and the decision had also been made that Groota would accompany the crew to Earth. After all the couple could return to Dooma at a later date. Perhaps Rosi would come along and continue her friendship with Bill. Bill grinned from ear to ear at the suggestion. Was this to be a planet to planet courtship??

The following morning the crew was invited to attend a history seminar at the school of higher learning [university]. Here they were introduced to Dr. Forge . He spoke of a time when Dooma was very concerned about the environment and what society was doing to destroy it. Global warming was also a very controversial subject and great efforts were made to curb it. Dooma also experienced ice ages and times when the ice receded. This went on for a decade before a brilliant scientist stated that all this was natural and that nature looked after itself. All the efforts being expended were for naught. The planet, including its oceans, was virtually cooling by about one degree per year. This was a normal cycle and had probably happened many times in the history of the planet. However it was a wake up call for society to be more efficient in the way they disposed of garbage and other waste products. Dr. Forge also suggested that Earth should change its ways of thinking and follow a similar pattern to Dooma. Apparently there had been a world-wide uproar when this discovery was made. Society had trusted the reports of the so-called experts and many unneeded changes were made, particularly in the industrial sector. In fact this was the beginning of the time of the big change on Dooma. There was a tremendous amount of good that came out of it in terms of the environment but most of it was not really necessary. Nature looks after itself. At least the Doomans were now aware of it and were able to assist nature in cleansing itself. It was also suggested that due to a certain changes in the celestial balance of the planets in our solar system changes in weather patterns on Earth could change.

Another theory with regard to global warming that was put forward at this seminar. Earth is not always in a constant orbit. It can vary so that the orbit takes on a more of an oval shape so that when it is at the greatest distance from the sun they will experience global cooling or an ice age. As the planets move back to a normal shaped orbit they are closer to the sun and thus experience global warming. This is a very gradual change so that there may be several millions of years between cycles. In Dooman scientific circles this theory made a lot of sense and, in fact, had been accepted in global studies.

As the crew went back to their quarters they saw that they had a great deal to consider in their reports to scientists back home. Of course there would be politicians to deal with as well. What kind of public outcry would come when this sort of information reached the media? Bill suggested that they make out a separate report and choose the proper time to release it. Keep it back until an appropriate time came up. Could it be that this would be the trigger to start changing the ways of the global society on Earth?

It has been noted that at a time of crisis people on Earth seem to forget their grievances and help each other out. Perhaps this is what it will take to make people realize the futility of war and decide to live in peace.

Dooma was not without natural disasters. There were volcanoes, hurricanes, tornados. floods, fires, and many other destructive events that resulted in loss of many lives and destruction of property. The Doomans coped with it as people on Earth do. They were not super beings any more than people on Earth. They had their fears and their other emotions that go along with life's struggles. The difference was that they had overcome the effects of greed and hostility. War was no longer an option. There was no need to strive for power because all the necessities of life were at hand. War efforts were transferred to peaceful endeavors and therefore all could enjoy the luxuries of life. In reality it would be with certain amount of regret that our crew from Earth would leave this planet.

Coming in for a landing

Moonbeam 3 Crew Plant Flag on Mars

Satellite Relay on Mars

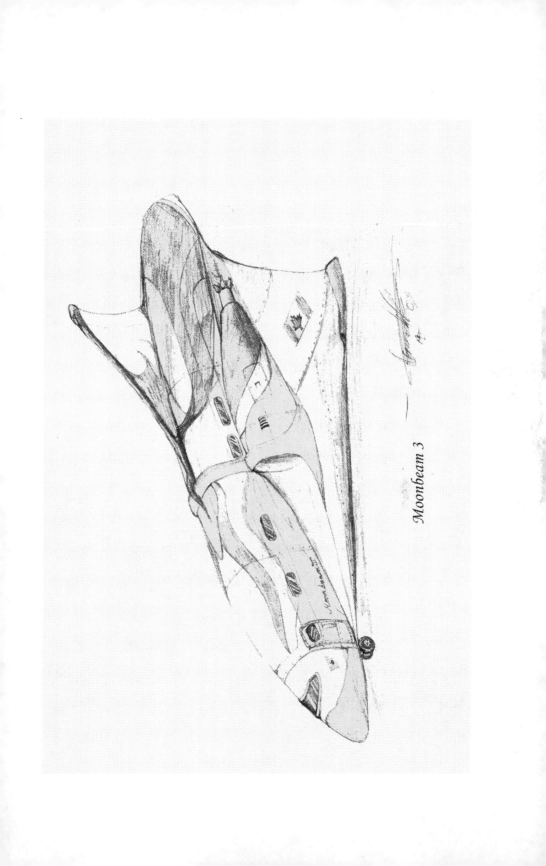

Moonbeam 3

Interior of Moonbeam 3

Astronaught In Flight Gear

Chapter Ten

The winter was cold and there was more than a foot of snow. As it dragged on the crew kept themselves busy socializing with their neighbors and continuing with their research. Sally and Groota were making plans for their wedding in the spring. Bill continued to keep company with Rosi although there were no suggestions of future wedding plans. They were all keeping daily records of their lives on this wonderful planet. They kept contact with home and all information about the new planet was to be kept secret until the return of Moonbeam and its famous crew. They considered it would be disastrous to let the media get hold of it and blow it out of proportion. The media on Dooma was much different in its approach to reporting events to the public. They did a good job of reporting but did not apply so much sensationalism to it. News was accurate and feats of heroism were fully recognized. Sports events were televised and the public was made aware of tragic events in a more modest manner. There was some advertising of new events and new products in the stores but it did not interrupt regular programming as it does on Earth. There was no money involved and competition was not a factor.

Now, as spring approached, Sally was taken in by a group of ladies, including Groota's mother. They were to prepare her for a Dooman wedding. What it amounted to was a huge feast attended by anybody who wanted to come. The food, which was supplied by the local food store, was prepared in a huge kitchen. The hall was decorated with bounteous amounts of fruits, vegetables, and flowers. It looked more like a thanksgiving festival celebrated on Earth. Betty's dress was that of a Dooman celebration as it was decorated with flowers and jewelry. She would wear a diamond studded crown on her head.

The excitement in camp rose as the great day approached. The other girls in the crew would accompany Betty to the place of marriage and stand with her during the ceremony. The men remained in the front row of the seating.

The final day arrived and they all arrived at the packed hall. Groota was already standing facing a very dignified look-ing gentleman. As the girls made their way up to the front a group of three pretty little girls sprinkled flower petals along the path in front of them. The gentleman in front of the couple muttered some words in Dooman and then in English shouted, "Good Luck", And that was it. Groota kissed Betty and they marched out arm in arm. Traditionally they would go to their new home and spend some time there before re-turning to the party. Because they would soon be on their way to Earth they went to a specially prepared house and carried on with tradition. When they arrived back they took their seats at the head of a long table and the feast was served. After dinner there was music, dancing, and a very nice program put on by the children. After this the children left and the party continued until after midnight. It was a wonderful day and the sun shone brightly on a very happy bride. Of course it was understood that there would be an Earth wedding soon after their arrival back home.

The most favorable time to leave on their homeward journey was on May 15, 3,024. They should arrive home in the spring of 3,026 Earth time. There was not too much preparation to do before leaving. Moonbeam was well stocked with food and supplies for the trip.

For some time Harry Good, the linguist had told Capt. Bill Williams that he would like to remain on Dooma and continue working with the language program. Bill had pretty well left it up to him. So, as the day approached, Harry wrote a formal request to stay. It was settled and Groota could take his place in the ship.

Two weeks before the projected time of departure Bill called a meeting of his crew and a couple of Dooman historians he had gotten to know. The purpose of the meeting was record a comprehensive report on their research findings over the past year. They had set up a large portable note board on which Bill could post headings and information could be recorded in a large log book to take back to Earth.

His first heading was, "Dooma before the big change". Under this heading were several sub-headings, the first being, "Conditions on the planet". There were terrible conditions on Dooma at this time. There were a number of countries at war and world-wide unrest prevailed as valuable land and factories were being destroyed by super bombs and chemical warfare. The war lords were living in luxury along with those producing war machines and war materials. These were mainly wars over religion, power struggles, and the right to rule. Children were being neglected and, in many cases, being taught to hate. Some of the children were taught to carry arms and fight whoever their parents were at odds with. There was wide-spread starvation in a land that could easily provide for all. Air, land, and water were being polluted at tragic levels. The planet was in a direct course to self- destruction. The people sensed this and there was unrest in all parts of Dooma. The politicians saw that something had to be done.

A council was formed including some very intelligent people, led by a man who was a very strong and convincing speaker. [e.g. Winston Churchill] He was able to get people to listen to him to bring about the "Big Change" The first quest was to bring all the war lords together and stop all wars. The word was broadcast that the planet had only five more years to survive. Every person on Dooma must come to terms with the situation or perish. Facing this, the people were willing to listen.

The first step after the wars stopped was to form a world council with two representatives from each country. Their task was to set the stage for the big change. One of the most difficult tasks was to convince the people that only one religion was necessary. They all worshipped a God and why not adopt one religion and then there would be nothing to fight over. This was a tough one so they gave it a period of ten years to be resolved. Language was another problem so the council decided that the best was to solve it would be to write a totally new language and that it would be used by all. Over a few generations the old languages would disappear. Perhaps the greatest thing to overcome was greed. The council reasoned that the planet could supply plenty for all so why would they need money? Goods could be distributed to central depots and the people could get what they needed. In place of making war materials all efforts could be directed to giving all people a high standard of living. Every family would be assured of a comfortable home and all that goes with it.

Now then did they really need politicians? This would be another tough sell but, after all, the alternative would be another power struggle. Each city or town would have a mayor invited to the position by the community. Each country had their two world councilors who were also selected by invitation. All problems were directed to the council and decisions were passed down to the mayor who was responsible for publicizing the information.

All this had happened a thousand years ago and of course there were growing pains but as the people realized the better way of life they were quite contented and went about their daily lives. They went to work, taking great pride in being Doomans and living a safe and carefree life.

The next heading Bill chalked onto the note board was; "Since the big change". This had the promise of being a long topic and they agreed to take a day's breather before continuing. They had to be sure to get all the details recorded in the correct sequence for their report.

Once again they got together with the two Dooman historians and got down to work covering each phase of the transition period from the time of disaster up to present time of peace and tranquility. From the start there were certainly growing pains. It must be remembered that the people had been thoroughly convinced that disaster lay ahead if they did not accept the changes and follow through with all the laws set out by the world council. Not all were in favor of the changes but, with overwhelming pressure from the majority, they eventually fell into line. Changing to a common religion was perhaps the last to be accepted. The change to a common language made everything much easier to deal with. In the first place it was a much simpler language and after a couple of generations the old dialects had pretty much disappeared. Amazingly once the money was taken out of circulation the desire for wealth and greed seemed to melt away. There was really no reason to fight for power because all goods were now available for all no matter what occupation the individual happened to be in. Advanced education was available to all so it was just a matter of choice of whatever the occupation was desired by the individual. This may seem to many readers to be a form of B.F. Skinner's "Walden Two". However it was a working example of a system that had worked for the Doomans for a thousand years. After two weeks of working on their report, all members of the crew were satisfied that they had done a thorough job and had a full report to take back to Earth.

The middle of May was fast approaching and it was time to prepare for their departure. Moonbeam was all cleaned up and ready for the long trip home. Groota was busy saying goodbye to all his friends and family and promising to come back for a visit. It just seemed as though he was going for a week's holiday; not the millions of miles he would be traveling.

At times Harry Good seemed to be a bit moody. Could it be that he was having second thoughts about staying behind. Bill had one last discussion with him about it but Harry assured him that he was determined to stay. If he got too homesick he might be able to hitch a ride in a Dooman ship. No more mention was made of it and, after all, Harry had made a lot of good friends here over the past year.

They knew there was going to be a huge farewell party before they left and so the date was set for May 14, 3114. Dignitaries started coming in from all parts of the planet. Most of the world council members were there to bid farewell to their friends from Earth. The whole area around the camp was decorated like a fairground. There were rides for the children and performing groups everywhere. There was a special stage set up for the main program of official farewells and a great feast was set out. The party actually lasted for two days and now the crew was all ready to go. On the morning of the 15ᵗʰ they gave moonbeam the last final check over and, with some modifications added by Gort and his crew, soundlessly left the ground. Under Betty's navigational guidance they were soon in orbit of Dooma. They made two orbits of Dooma to take last photographs and then set course for home. Expected time of arrival was about the middle of May a year hence.

Chapter Eleven

As Moonbeam was gathering speed Sally set the course for home. They would go to meet Earth in her own orbit of the Sun. In two days time Moonbeam would be up to cruising speed. Now the crew could settle in for the long trip. Groota and Betty had their own little room provided for in the renovation before take-off. Now the crew had plenty of time to reflect upon their historic experiences. They all vowed that they would make a return trip to Dooma at some time. They had thousands of pictures to show people at home and toyed with the idea of making a movie to help pay for the next trip.

One evening, as they were playing cards, Dr. Morgan remarked, "You know, none of us even had so much as a cold all the time we were away. Wouldn't it be wonderful to have the Dooman system set up on Earth? Maybe Groota can help us to develop their system of disease control". Groota said that he was on the team that built their system and that he could always communicate with Gort if he needed any help.

There was so much to learn!! The extensive use of power from the sun, e.g. the solar heating system for all buildings, electric power, and the harnessing of magnetic force for locomotion. All this and to live where there is no conflict and little or no crime.

Jane remarked, "What a wonderful place to bring up children! Just think of it! No video parlors and no smutty shows on TV! Just look at what we are going home to". All gave a deep sigh and Bill asked, "Shall we turn around and go back to Dooma? They all laughed and agreed that they had better continue on their journey.

About a month into their journey Betty asked to have a private talk with Dr.Tom. She confided in him that she was pregnant. He congratulated her and remarked, "I have never heard of a space ship having a maternity ward nor a baby being born in space but I suppose there is a first for everything. Now don't you worry! We will be able to look after you and we will adjust". He added, "I think we will have to tell the others, don't you"? Groota was a very proud father-to-be. He was a little bit apprehensive about it but had confidence in Dr. Tom. When the crew heard the news they all applauded and decided it was time to crack a bottle of good Dooman wine. Putting the card game aside they all toasted the couple and spent a late night in song and laughter. All was well aboard Moonbeam.

Sally continued her job as navigator and along with Fred Wong, she continued to take sightings of other stars and create a navigational map for later probes into space. They never ceased to wonder at the beauty of the stars from their unimpeded vantage point. They were like diamonds in the sky.

One day, to break the monotony Bill asked Groota what he knew about prehistoric life on Dooma. Groota told him that he had studied that very topic at their higher school of learning.[University] Apparently Dooma had three known ice ages when glacier invaded half way down to the equator. He told them that Doomans went through the same stages of evolution as humans on Earth. During the stone-age they lived in caves and fought savage battles over food supplies, women, and territorial rights. They were rugged creatures and as time progressed so did their weapons. By the time of the big change Doomans were fighting full scale wars. Basically there were four continents and thousands of islands. Each continent and surrounding islands had their own language and their own religious beliefs. Groota said that their scientists had traced human life back over five million years and that during the ice ages only those living in the tropics had survived. To put it in a nutshell Dooma had gone through the same stages as Earth. There is no doubt that Dooma was the result of an outburst of the sun, the same as all the other planets.

The next question was whether there had been dinosaurs roaming Dooma. Groota said that some strange looking fossils had been dug up but nothing like those unearthed on planer Earth. There were some creatures that were said to survive the prehistoric times but the most important survivors were the Doomans themselves.

It was now September and all was well on Moonbeam. Betty was definitely showing her pregnancy. She had gone through a brief spell of morning sickness but otherwise was doing fine. Dr. Tom was keeping her under his watchful eye and told her to expect to give about mid April. This would make the baby a month old when they set down on Earth. All members of the crew were looking forward to the arrival of a new crew member.

By now Dooma was no longer visible from Moonbeam and Earth was in full view. From out in space it was easy to see the relationship of the planets and their moons with the sun. All was in order to make up our days and all the seasons making up a year. This would certainly be an ideal position to be in for those studying astrology. As Moonbeam came closer to

Earth the crew could now make out the continents and oceans on Earth. It was truly a welcome sight,

On the fourteenth of April Betty woke with some strange feelings, a sort of pressure in her back. Yes, this was the early stages of labor pains and De. T told the crew to get ready for the cry of a baby. All members of the crew pitched in to make everything ready for the birth. Curtains were placed around the bed in the main cabin and lights were placed to make up a pretty good operating room. As the pains became more frequent Dr. T got all his gear ready and did his final scrub for the birth. Bill asked Groota to come forward just to get the excited father out of the way. He gave Groota some unnecessary navigational problem to solve just to keep his mind off what was going on with his wife. At the right moment Dr. T called Groota back to witness the birth. It wasn't long before there came the first cry from the baby girl. Dr. T examined the baby and told the couple they had a perfectly normal child. After everything was cleared up, the baby looked after; they all cheered and drank a toast to the Dooma family.

Now there was a minor complication; the matter of naming the child. On Dooma a child was given a name but there was no family name. Each family had a family crest in the form of a brass broach worn by the father. His wife had her own family crest and when she married she was presented with a replica of her husband's crest. Wearing two crests identified her as a married woman. When a bay was born he/she was presented with a tiny replica of the fathers crest. Consequently all of the Doomans were called by their given names. Now, on Earth, how were Grooten and Betty going to handle the situation. The simplest way would be to give Grooten a family name. Grooten had a solution. He would take full Earth names and not bother with the name Grooten. In that way their daughter would have a first name as well as a family name. So it was decided to change Grooten's first name to James and his family name to Simon. Now Betty would be Mrs. Simon. Of course this would all be done legally on Earth. They would name the baby Susie which was also a Dooman name.

There was another item that Betty wanted Grooten [Jim] to change and that was his wardrobe. On Dooma all the men wore loose fitting trousers tied in at the cuffs. There was no crease in them. They wore loose blouse-like shirts, usually very brightly colored. Betty asked Grooten, "How would you like to be dressed in a suit with a tie". He replied, "I will do anything to please you my dear". You see, he had picked up the English language very well along with the dutiful words of an earthly husband.

All crew members would have a very good pay cheque to come home to because they had not drawn any pay while they were away. They had talked about where they would settle down once they arrived at the base where they had left from. They agreed that they would get homes in the same neighborhood so that they could visit back and forth. After all, they planned to continue their careers in space research.

Part Two

Readers must be reminded that this story is strictly fiction although most of us may hope that it could be true. The possibility of the following events becoming reality may be remote but it is the opinion of the author that this is the route that must be taken to save our planet. For the sake of simplicity this part of the story will take place in a Canadian locale where ordinary people live and raise their families in reasonable comfort. Employment is steady and salaries are average for the time.

Chapter Twelve

Sally Post was doing a wonderful job of plotting the route back to Earth. Capt. Bill Williams kept the ship right on course and as they neared Earth Moonbeam would have to start slowing down for the final decent. If they came in too fast the ship would overheat and possibly burn up. When they were three days out Bill started the retro jets and very slowly allowed the ship to lose speed, this was necessary to prevent discomfort to the crew. Now they could make out the oceans and continents. The moon was on the opposite side of the earth so this would not interfere with their approach. Into their last day the ship had slowed to the speed of a fast jet and would be safe to enter the atmosphere of Earth.

They now came under direct control from the main control center where they would land. Bill guided the ship to a hover position directly over the landing pad. With his usual skill he brought Moonbeam down onto the pad with a slight bump. They were safely home. Dr. Tom Morgan instructed the crew to very cautiously take their first breath of home air. It was particularly important for Jim [Groota] because it would be a first for him. Moonbeam was quickly moved into a hanger and a security guard put in place. As they disembarked each took a sniff of Earth air. Jim took a small sniff and remarked that the smell was not like the air on Dooma. It didn't have that sweet smell of home. However he accepted it and felt no ill effects from it.

There were quite a number of dignitaries to welcome the travelers home. Cameras were flashing but reporters were not allowed to speak to any members of the crew. This would come after all debriefing was completed and then there would be a press release allowed. The crew was ushered into a nearby hotel where they were assigned quarters where they must stay until after all their reports were in and they were given permission to leave. Betty and Jim were given an executive suite with all services open to them. There was even a crib provided for little Susie.

The next morning the crew was invited to the main lecture room for debriefing. Each, in turn, gave a full report on their findings on the new found planet. This turned out to be a week-long process. Added to that, there was another two day period for questions. A camera crew was present but the media was kept out. They already knew about the discovery of the new planet and the return of the crew. They would just have to wait for the officials to allow them access to these famous astronauts. They made many attempts to gain access to the hotel but it was very well secured.

The reports were very well presented and at last the members of the crew were allowed some freedom. Their first idea was to buy cars so they could get around. Just as they were about to leave Betty said to Jim, "Now hold it Jim. You are going to get into some Earth clothes before we do anything else". "Anything you say my dear". You see! He was learning to be an earthling already.

They proceeded to the mall and found a men's shop. They picked out a very nice suit, tie, and some shirts. On leav-

ing the store Jim walked right past the till without paying for
his clothes. Betty called him back and said, 'you have to pay
money for goods here". Of course he was used to just picking
up what he wanted on Dooma. They had a bit of a laugh over
it and then proceeded to a car dealership. They bought a neat
little hybrid car and on the way back to the hotel Jim said,
"Why don't we call our car Moonbeam 2"? "What a wonderful idea", replied Betty and they both laughed.

At the hotel they all gathered for dinner and exchanged
notes of their doings for the day. They had all bought new
cars and a couple of them had looked at houses. Fred Wong
said that he was amazed at some of the changes that had taken
place since they left. Some of the new homes were completely
solar powered and heated.

On the political side some advanced ideas were going
ahead. The wars in the Middle East had been brought to a
temporary cease fire while all nations had been called to a
world peace conference. A world council had been set up with
two delegates from each nation. A very strong spoken and
persuasive spokesperson had been selected to speak on behalf
of the council. As those conflicts were basically over differences in religious beliefs, the suggestion was put forth that all
people should conform to one religion. After all, they all worship a God and why fight over the method of worship? This
was taken on advisement and it was obvious that this would
be a hard nut to crack. At least the seed had been planted and
there seemed to be a glimmer of hope that the wars would
come to an end. At least, those involved seemed very willing
to listen. There would have to be meaningful meetings of religious leaders with the resolve to make it work.

By this time the members of the crew were settled in
their homes. Fred Wong and Dr. Tom were now married and

looking forward to raising families. Betty was pregnant again and Jim was enjoying his life on Earth. He was working as a consultant and at the present time was working with the forestry people to change their ways of harvesting the trees. A factory was under construction to produce building material such as was used on Dooma.

Eliminating the monetary system would probably take a whole generation for acceptance; possibly more. The problem of distribution of goods would have to be solved and honed to be sure there was plenty for all. The resources were there but the money hungry financiers favored the wealthy and the poor were left without even the essentials of living in comfort. If all people were to live with dignity they had to have equal opportunity to share the bounty of the earth. It may take several generations to expel greed from the lives of the people. This would obviously have to be started at a very young age. The entire education system would have to be changed; not only for children but adults as well. Educators would have to be trained before progress could even be started. Language specialists had already started working on a universal language. To make this worldwide would probably take at least two generations. Removing power seeking politicians may not be possible until the monetary system had been expelled. It may be wondered what initiative would make people want to work at all. The incentive would have to be survival and pride in accomplishment at the work place. The latter must be taught at a very young age be it at school or later when entering the work force. The Doomans were taught personal pride in being Doomans. This is what Doomans did and their reward was a carefree and secure lifestyle. Most of the stress was removed from the work place. It must be remembered that the Doomans only worked four hour shifts. There was not that drive to make more money.

At the time of the return of our astronauts the drug trade was outpacing the law and was completely out of control. If there was no money the drugs would cease to be of value to the drug lords. Certainly there would be those who still wanted drugs for their own consumption but this could be controlled through intensive anti-drug education in the home and at school. The next generation would not even know that drugs existed. The savings to policing and to the medical system would be enormous. As happened on Dooma, the crime rate fell to a point that policing was hardly necessary.

Pornography and sex programming would have to be totally removed from the media, computers, video machines, and any other place where it was now displayed. In fact, the video parlors would just as well be done away with altogether. This is where young children grew up with driving cars at breakneck speed, weaving in and out of traffic. After a number of years on these machines they would try the same stunts when they started to drive real cars. They would have to learn from the start that driving a car is not a right but a privilege.

Smoking could soon be eliminated by taking cigarettes and all other smoking materials off the market altogether. What a boon to the medical system!! Cancer and many other illness could be reduced and maybe eliminated. If a child never saw a cigarette it is very unlikely that he/she would ever have the desire to smoke.

One might ask what would take the place of these so-called pleasures. In the schools children would be introduced to many other enjoyable activities to pass the time of play. Non-violent sports, music, books, board games, and just playing with friends and pets. In the past farm children grew up with plenty to keep themselves busy. They started at a very young age helping with chores and going to school. Most of them came through without getting into trouble with the law. Idleness is one of the major causes of delinquency and mischievous behavior. Surely if a society can spend billions on producing war materials they can supply our children with suitable entertainment and recreational material.

All these things were placed in the hands of world council to find solutions. It was up to these people to choose acceptable solutions and pass them on down to each country for implementation. This is a very large goal to try to achieve and it is not surprising that it took over a century for Dooma to come to their present stage. Saving a planet from self destruction is not an easy task and in order to make it work the people must be made aware of what is happening and be driven almost to a state of panic in order to get them to comply with the required changes. People are stubborn and some have been known to ignore warnings of an approaching hurricane and perish rather than taking cover.

Some scientists have predicted that there is a meteorite about the size of Australia in a direct flight path for our solar system. If it should strike the earth it would be a disaster beyond all comprehension. There would be a pall of dust that would block out the sun for at least five years. Life as we know it would cease and the earth's orbit could be affected as well as its axis so that the seasons would be thrown out of kilter. On the other hand it could land on any of the other planets including Dooma. It would just depend on the position of the planets in their orbits around the sun. It may even be pulled into the sun by its gravitational pull and cause little or no effect on the planets. This meteorite is so far away that it might take as long as fifteen years to get here. If, at the time, our scientist did determine that it would land on Earth and they couldn't devise a way of diverting it there would certainly be widespread panic. The only way to prevent this would be if those who knew of it kept it under cover and it would happen so fast that nobody would know about it anyhow. This, of course, is just one of those suppositions. If, however, this sort of information, perhaps by a terrorist, were released to the media as fact, could cause utter chaos

Chapter Thirteen

The next five years passed with great strides being made in an attempt to model after the planet Dooma. One startling change involved Jim. He and Betty now had two children; Susie and a baby boy. They were perfectly normal children it was difficult to keep them out of the limelight. People were just curious and called them the kids from outer space.

Jim was working on a new pilot project to develop air purification following the system on Dooma. Conferring with Gort, he got the formula for the disinfectant used back home and experimentally filled a pressurized tank truck with the mixture. At night when there was no traffic the truck went up and down the streets spraying a fine mist of the solution. It had the same sweet smell as the crew noticed when they took their first breath of air on Dooma. It was absolutely harmless to all creatures that breathed air. This was purely experimental and on a very small scale and it would take time to show any results. After six months it was noted that nobody had colds during that time and there was a marked drop in the number of patients in the local hospital.

Another project was the development of a city center heating system using solar heat. Jim was the consultant who led the city engineers in this project. The first thing that had to be done was to build the solar heat plant. It was capable of storing huge volumes of hot air compressed in large vessels buried deep in the earth. They were cacooned in very efficient insulating material. The next step was to bury pipe wrapped with the same insulation and there was one supply pipe into each home. It distributed the heat through the house heating system and could be controlled by thermostats in the houses. In the first year two streets were used for test purposes. This pilot project worked so well that the city voted to have it used city wide. This would eliminate the use of natural gas and reduce air pollution in a very big way. The cost to consumers would be much cheaper as well and of course when they got rid of the monetary system it would be free. Now engineers came from all over the world to study this program.

Getting out of the monetary system faced huge opposition from the people with money. The big cry was, "We worked hard for our money and now we are being asked to give it up". What they were afraid of was giving up their power over others. They couldn't understand that they could have anything they wanted without flashing their wealth around. Much of the stress in the workplace would be gone. They only needed to work half time and have more time to enjoy life. This change would not likely happen until the younger generation move up. The world council on Dooma faced the same problems and it took over a century to get it working.

One day When Jim came home from work Betty was in a huge state of excitement. She had heard that a Dooman space ship was coming for a visit. One member of the crew would be Susi, Bill's friend. She said she had just been talking to the Captain. "Guess who the Captain is!!" she screamed. "It is Gort and he is going to stay with us". Jim said, "We must get over to Bill's place and let him know right away".

The whole crew met at Bill's place that night. Apparently Bill knew all about the visit from Dooma. After all he had kept in touch with Susi and would carry on a serious courtship when she got here. The ship was due in three days. The party that night lasted until 2:00 am.

The Moonbeam crew had continued with their training to keep up with the advances in space technology. They were planning another journey into space for the next spring. They wanted to explore the other side of Mars. Would they find yet another inhabited planet? This time they would be traveling in a new super space ship, Moonbeam 3. It could reach even faster speeds than their first ship. Of course the children wanted to go along with Betty and Jim but this would be a five year trip and the children would have to be in school. They would be in the care of a very competent nanny and Betty's mother and father lived only a block away.

Betty said to Jim, "If Bill and Susi are going to get married it would be a good time for us to have our Earth wedding". Jim replied with a big hug, "What a wonderful idea! I have been thinking about that for some time now". Jim wondered if they would be able to stop off at Dooma on their way to Mars. They would have to ask Bill about that. After all he would be the captain on the new trip. In fact all the crew members wanted to hold their original positions. Another passenger coming from Dooma was Harry Good. Of course he would join the crew on the new adventure.

At last the great day came when the first UFO [from Dooma] arrived and all the crew members of Moonbeam were there to greet them. They were among the celebrities to welcome the visitors. It was easy to see that Bill had kept up his romance with Susi as they embraced and the tears of joy ran down Susi's face. The ship from Dooma was quickly brought into the special space hanger and after all the introductions the guests were ushered to the same hotel where they too would stay until after the debriefing was done. There was a crew of eight plus the two passengers, Susi and Harry. All members spoke English fluently; thanks to Harry. There were two Dooma techs along to help out with some of the technical projects that were now already started. It was much easier having these engineers on hand rather than using radio communication from Dooma.

Once the debriefing and medical checks were done the guests were taken to the homes of the Moonbeam crew. They all gathered at Mary Swan's place for the welcome feast. The weather was perfect and they had a bbq of good Alberta beef steaks and all the good stuff prepared by Mary. It was a wonderful party and all the talk was about the two up-coming weddings. It was now official that Bill and Susi would indeed be married and that Susi would stay on Earth with Bill. She was a little dismayed when she heard about the space trip that would be taking off in a month's time,

It would take some time for the weddings to be prepared for so they set the wedding date for June 1st, 3122. It now was official that Moonbeam 3 would take flight on June 28, 3122. To the surprise of everyone Bill announced that Susi had taken space travel training and would be a new member of his crew. All were overjoyed at the news.

The Dooman crew was invited to an official welcome by the city and once again was treated to a great feast. They were absolutely thrilled to see Alberta beef on the menu. They said they had never tasted such delicious meat back home.

The two Dooman techs were assigned to the engineers who were working on the solar heating project and were prepared to help out wherever they could. The amazing thing was that they didn't expect any pay for their work. However they would be treated like royalty and they certainly didn't have to pay for anything either.

Susi stayed with Jim and Betty waiting for the great day. The two brides had a wonderful time picking out their wedding dresses and all the other preparations that have to be done. The grooms got fitted with tuxes and had wonderful time getting ready. Groota was now staying at Bill's place and of course the other male crew members spent a lot of time there too. Jim Bolder would be Bill's best man and Fred Wong would look after Groota. Sally Post would be Betty's maid of honor and Toni Janske would be Susi's maid of honor. The other girls would serve as bride's maids for both the brides.

At last the big day came with bright sunshine and the smell of fresh flowers in the air. This would be a traditional service in one of the city's big Churches to be performed by a minister. The brides looked stunning as they came down the aisle. The two couples were married at the same time and the ceremony was followed by a trip to the photographers and a wonderful reception in the community hall. There were only fifty invited guests because they didn't want to be plagued with questions about space.

Now all members of the crew were married and settled in their new homes. They took up the Canadian lifestyle while at home but earnestly worked at their training to man the new spacecraft Moonbeam 3. It was a beauty; a little roomier than Moonbeam 1 and had much more technical apparatus on board. For example it had a much more powerful telescope and improved camera equipment. They wanted to get as much outer space information as possible. The eyes of the world were on these adventursome astronauts and all wished them well.

Chapter Fourteen

After a hearty feast and party the crew was all set to board Moonbeam 3 and set out on another epic journey. Just as the sun was peeping over the horizon Moonbeam 3 took flight into an easy orbit around Earth. Once again Sally Post took over the navigation duties. Captain Bill Williams at the controls set the ship into a steady acceleration. It would take only two weeks to gain maximum cruising speed. He set the course into Earth's orbit as they went to meet Dooma. They loved the roominess of their new home as they floated along in weightlessness. Being seasoned astronauts they fell into their regular routine, each carrying on with their assigned duties. Bill didn't have to stay at the controls all the time because the ship was set on course and required very little adjustment. They were all familiar with the controls and took turns in the control seat.

Susi and Groota [Jim] were quite excited about going home and telling their friends and families about their Earth adventure.. The others were also looking forward to renewing their friendships from their previous visit. This trip was more relaxing because they knew where they were going and what they would find. The months just seemed to fly by and the first thing they knew they were into their second year. The sight of Dooma peeping around the sun was a welcome sight. At three months before touch-down they were met by three Dooma spacecraft to welcome them back.

When they touched down at their old site the welcoming party was there. Their quarters in the Dooma house were all in order and the kitchen was well stocked with food, The shelter for Moonbeam 3 had to be enlarged a bit and that was done the next day. Bill had to inform them that they would not be staying long because they were on a much longer mission.

The crew went through another debriefing and they were brought up to date on what had been going on in Dooma. Of course the Doomans were very curious to know how the big change was progressing on Earth. Having dispensed with all of this the crew just took it easy and enjoyed their surroundings on this beautiful planet. Bill and Susi and Betty and Groota spent time with their respective families. As they prepared to continue their journey they pored over astral maps with Dooma space captains who were quite familiar with the trip to Mars.

There was the opportunity for at least two members of the crew to stay behind but they all wanted to go. So it was that they all boarded Moonbeam 3 and were on their way to Mars. They knew that if they landed on Mars they would have to wear all their space gear because the atmosphere here would not support life. They were more interested in what they would see on the other side of Mars; another hidden planet perhaps. This was a very long journey because they had to chase down Mars and then orbit around to the far side.

This time they could see their objective all the way. Mars is somewhat smaller than Earth so that the gravitational pull would be less than that of Earth. As they drew in closer to Mars they could see how barren it looked with no trees or other vegetation. There was no visible sign of water so that no living thing could survive there. Moonbeam 3 handled beautifully as they came in for a landing on a nice level spot. Before alighting the crew donned their space suits which included oxygen tanks for breathing. One by one they made their way to the escape hatch. One would move into the chamber and after the door was sealed shut, would slide out and onto the ground. This exercise was repeated until they were all out. There really wasn't much they could do here but take pictures and some soil samples to take back home. They were noticeably lighter here than on Earth or Dooma and they had a bit of fun gliding along hardly touching the ground. They found a cave in the side of an outcropping of rock. A couple of them went inside but found nothing of interest. There was certainly no sign of life and there was no water either.

Bill cautioned the others not to stay too long because they only had a limited amount of oxygen. They returned to the ship and took their turn at going aboard. They had their lunch there and spent some time taking pictures. While out, they took great pleasure in placing a Canadian flag on a knoll marking the first people from Earth to set foot on the planet. Dooman astronauts had been there before them but no others that were known of.

The crew decided to stay where they were until the next morning and then take off for their orbit of Mars. Now this was not a very exhilarating trip because they found no other planet behind Mars. They did, however, get some very good photographs of the different landscapes and also positions of many more stars.

They made three different orbits around Mars so were able to map it out pretty well. Bill set the ship down one more time to install a radio beam forwarding device so that Earth scientists could have their own communication system with Dooma. They were all relieved to turn Moonbeam 3 toward home.

Chapter Fifteen

The journey home would not be without interruption. Into their second month as they were cruising along Susi said to Bill, "Do you think we could stop off at Dooma? There is something I forgot to bring with me". Bill, "Well dear, it is not that far out of our way. Yes dear, we will stop off but not for more than a week. There is a lot of work to be done when we get home". Sally radioed in for landing clearance and the next day they were being escorted in by two Dooman craft. It was a wonderful sight to see the green of a living planet.

Bill brought Moonbeam 3 in for a flawless landing and there was Susi's family waiting to greet them. As they arrived at her home Bill asked her, "By the way! What was it that you forgot to bring"? She said, "It was my identification broaches. I don't feel right without them". Bill said, "Oh Susi! You don't really need them on Earth. I have already told you that you will go by the name of Mrs. Williams". He chuckled, "Let's enjoy a good week of rest now we are here". They all had a good laugh over it and no more was said.

The other members of the crew were back in the Dooma house just relaxing. Bill checked with home base once a day to see how the plan was working and of course other members contacted their families at home. All were doing fine. The

Earth communication on Mars was working perfectly. Bill commented that he didn't want to have to go back there any time soon. As they were preparing to leave they knew what was coming. There would be another big farewell party put on by their Dooman friends. These people certainly did enjoy party time.

The crew wound up staying for ten days before going on board and heading for Earth. They were not taking very much new scientific data back with them but they considered the trip was worthwhile. Besides, it was a good test for Moonbeam 3. They now felt that they had a very reliable and safe space ship. They had tested out new instruments and photographic equipment and, above all, they had installed the communication unit on Mars. They had tested it from Dooma and communication experts had given it a number one rating.

To pass the time all of the crew members spent a couple of hours a day studying the new language they would soon be using on Earth. This was the language they used in every day conversation and by the time they reached Earth they were quite fluent in it. It reminded them of their first days on Dooma when they were trying to communicate with the people there.

It was now five years since Moonbeam left Earth and as it approached home base everything was working perfectly. This time the debriefing session and medical inspections were quite short. Dr. Tom reported that he had nothing to report. There hadn't been so much as a runny nose on the whole trip. They knew there would not likely be any contamination from Mars and that Dooma had already proven to be clean.

The crew members were very quickly back in their own homes and telling of their adventures in outer space. The children had grown from babies to youngsters, some already in pre-school. The schools were already adopting some of the new ways of teaching the children. They were not learning a second foreign language but the new universal language. Great headway was being made to convert other countries. As mentioned before, it had to work.

The people were struggling a bit with the new language and were trying to use it in every day conversation. Workers were getting used to a four hour working day and enjoying the extra time with family. Changing the way of shopping would not be easy. People were used to selecting what they wanted and then paying for it at the cash register. They looked for sale items and, in many cases, lined up for hours to get a bargain. The first test store, a grocery store, opened its doors for the "no money" trial. Of course people flocked there in record breaking crowds. They pushed and shoved to get in the doors. There was a large staff of clerks there to tell them that there was no rush and to take their time. All they had to do was to load what they needed into a shopping cart and then go to the check-out. The goods were run through a scanner for stock control purposes only and the customers went on their way. They were told not to hoard stuff because the shelves would be full again tomorrow. Anybody wanting further instruction on how the system worked could join special classes and many took advantage of this service.

This program was run for a month and was advertised as a huge success. Soon other businesses were making inquiries about the system and very soon all money was withdrawn from the city. The people were completely bewildered as it became more acceptable they started to understand the merit of it. All money was turned in and recorded at the banks and the people were assured that, provided they co-operated, they would soon see how the system would work. Managers and supervisors took a lot of convincing that they would no longer receive pay checks. The ordinary workers accepted the change much more readily and welcomed in the four hour day. Business owners and professional people were a hard sell but with certain guarantees they soon responded favorably. The system gradually spread across the globe, sporadically at first and then, as it caught on, grew to world-wide acceptance. It had taken only ten years of concentrated publicity and learning seminars in all areas in preparation for the first trial run. As on Dooma there were plenty of growing pains but as the next generation moved into position the whole concept became acceptable and the people were happy with it.

All the main administrative organizations of the cities remained in place except that the administrators were hired on the basis of their expertise rather than by means of political campaigns. In other words there were no longer any politicians. The world council was the governing body and, as previously mentioned, they were appointed; two from each country. A huge administrative force was required to carry out all the directives from the main council.

How could all this be possible?? Not easy! It must be understood that most human activities are learned and therefore if the teachings are standardized very positive results can be achieved. This does not take away the introduction of new ideas by individuals so long as these ideas are productive and fit into the scheme of things. The ability to think and invent new concepts is not taken away; in fact it is encouraged. Under this system it would not be possible for terrorist types to rise to power. From the cradle people are taught to do what is right and all temptation to do otherwise has been removed. The skeptics will certainly say, "Rubbish"!! But this is what has to be done to save our planet from self destruction. [Correction], human destruction]. All corruption has been caused by man and man must undo this corruption. There are enough natural disasters on Earth to deal with without creating more. Until all people realize this there is very little that can be done but wait for that day when all the lights go out.

The time had come for our astronauts to take on a different role. Certainly they would still be associated with space travel and exploration of the stars we see in our skies. Every one of them was a space specialist and could now take consulting positions. They were always in high demand for public presentations in the community and particularly in the schools and universities. Groota, "the man from outer space" was particularly in demand. That curiosity about space and the planets grew with each new discovery. More and more students wanted to get into space science. With the knowledge of the common DNA of Doomans and Earth people the door was now wide open for going even deeper into our origin. Were Darwin's theories of evolution viable? There isn't really anything in those new discoveries that would that would dispute them. After all we are considering millions of years of evolution and we know that it continues today. How many new viruses have been discovered, even in the last decade? Were they here before? We don't really know what may lie ahead. New organisms could develop into a new age of monsters like the dinosaurs. We cannot even be sure that humans have reached their final destiny. It has been suggested that in time we will take up a stance of sitting in front of a computer and cease to have the ability to walk. Our youth must be encouraged to exercise and build strong bodies. Most could stand to shed a few pounds of fat as well.

Thanks to the crew of Moonbeam, the people on Earth have a sample to follow. There may be flaws in Dooma world but, at least, they have averted the disaster that faces planet Earth unless similar changes are made here. If they were to stick to the plan, the only thing that could destroy Earth would be one of nature's natural disasters. People could now live a secure life without the fear of wars or even terrorism that has been growing in their own communities. There would be no more power struggles and greed could eventually be a thing of the past. The stress of living costs requiring both parents to work could change to a more leisurely life style. The children would be raised at home thus doing away with the need for daycare services. Is this Utopia? It is here for us if we are willing to make the changes.

Chapter Sixteen

The debriefing reports from each of the astronauts give a cross-section of the accomplishments of the two missions into space. They are recorded here individually. It will be noted that there is not one complaint about the whole operation.

Captain Bill Williams: The crews of Moonbeam 1 and Moonbeam 3 worked very well as teams. All were of a same mind as to the legitimate reasons for their missions. They were all sure that they would find a new planet on the other side of the sun. When it was discovered they showed little surprise and were overjoyed at their discovery. We were even more thrilled to find that Dooma was inhabited by intelligent beings. As we explored the planet we were even more astounded at the way the Doomans had solved all the problems that threatened to destroy their existence there.

Both ships operated flawlessly and brought us safely back from each of our excursions. At this point I want to thank our hosts for their friendship and willingness to help us with our missions. Their hospitality will never be forgotten. Of course you all know that myself and Betty are now married to Doomans and, in fact, Betty has two children from her Dooman husband. In conclusion I would like to thank the media for using restraint when we asked for it. It is the wish of all the crew that the people of our planet will take up the challenge and bring about peaceful lives for all.

Sally Post: As navigator of both ships I want to express my thanks to those who put Moonbeam 1 and Moonbeam 2 together and the care they took to make sure the crew members would be as comfortable as possible. Both ships operated perfectly and, as you can see, brought us safely home.. I wish to thank the Doomans for their hospitality and especially to Gort and Groota for their help with the communications. It was an exhilarating experience to go into the Dooman homes and see how they raised their children. Lastly I would like to thank all members of the crew for co-operating in such a wonderful way.

Dr. Tom Morgan: I don't have very much to report with regard to the crew. They were in superb health when we left and I didn't see even a runny nose on either trip. We learned a great deal from our hosts on Dooma and I will be giving a detailed report to medical officials here. We have a great deal to learn from them. I might add that we have brought back some herb plants to cultivate here. These herbs are the link we have been searching for in our search for a cure for cancer. I want to take this opportunity to thank the Dooman medical staff for all the information they gave us.

Harry Good: As interpreter for the mission my first meeting with the Doomans was a bit intimidating. However I was amazed at how quickly they were able to grasp what we were trying to say to them. They have a very good sense of humor and are very eager to learn. As a matter of fact I enjoyed teaching them [and learning from them] so much that I asked Captain Bill if I could stay behind and continue my work when Moonbeam 1 returned to Earth. My wish was granted and I feel that it was a good decision because we accomplished a great deal while I was there. The Doomans in my classes gained enough of the English language to be able to communicate reasonably well. Now we have our new language I suppose I will have to go back there and start lessons all over again. Believe me: I'm ready to go any time. I also wish to thank Bill for holding the crew together and making those long days and nights a pleasure while we were in space. The close confinement didn't seem to do any of us any harm.

Jim Bolder: These last few years of travel and adventure have been an experience that none of us will ever forget. Part of my job was gathering samples of the Dooma plant life. We were able to bring back quite a bit of it, thanks to the designers of Moonbeam 1. The large storage bin at the rear of the ship was big enough for the soil samples as well. Our plants and seedlings will get the best of care in our new greenhouse. I want to thank those who built this wonderful facility for us. We will be able to get right to work analyzing the samples we brought back

Jane Silver: I agree with all of you that it was a very successful adventure and every member of the crew contributed to its success. I want to thank all of you for making my housekeeping job an easy one. After we arrived on Dooma I had a great desire to find out how the family life worked. I spent many days in their homes and marveled at how they cared for their children. There were no disturbing toys of violence. Man and wife seemed to live in perfect harmony. There was no divorce or separation. One interesting thing that I did notice was that each one of them had a private room to themselves in the house. If one of them wanted some time out, the other one took charge of the children he/she could go to his/her room just to be alone for awhile. They agreed that this saved many family clashes from ever being an issue. Thank you again and I'm ready to go again anytime.

Fred Wong: As a scientist I must say that the trip to Dooma satisfied all the criteria for modern research. We were very fortunate to find that the new planet was populated and that we were able to communicate with them. It will take months to go through all the testing and experiments with all the samples we brought back with us. Dooma has opened up a whole new chapter in science for us. If it can save our planet from disaster then everything that went into this program is more than worthwhile. I want to thank all of you for helping gather these valuable samples and particularly to Captain Williams for keeping the schedule according to plan.

Betty Simms: I suppose that my report will lead us a little bit off the track of our objective. As you know I had a great deal of work to do in the communication room. Being out of range of radio signals from Earth placed a certain amount of anxiety on all of us as well as those at home. Thanks to the help from Gort and Groota we were able to solve the problem. This led to the establishment of a permanent radio station on Mars. This gives us space-wide radio communication in seconds.

I don't know if you would call this part of the research program but as you know I worked with Groota and as fate would have it we fell in love. It became obvious that this was going to be a lasting relationship and the question came up, "What if we have children"? This led to a scurry of research in the field of genetics involving DNA. It was discovered that we were compatible and we could have normal children. And to end a happy story Groota and I are now married and have two beautiful children and are living here on Earth. Incidentally, we discovered that DNA is far more widespread than we could ever imagine. This will all come out in future reports from the medical sciences people   I am also very grateful to the members of both Moonbeam crew for your co-operation during this historic adventure.

Mary Swan: Fellow astronauts;   It was a privilege for me to be a member of the crew on this fabulous journey. I was very happy to find that none of you were fussy eaters. I learned a great deal from the Dooma cooks and will continue to use some of their recipes here on Earth. Their foods are not that different from our own and they certainly know how to cater to a party. To anybody who goes to that wonderful place, be prepared for a big feast when you get there or leave. The Doomans are the friendliest people I have ever met and I look forward to the next opportunity to go back again.

Toni Janske: This was a geologist's dream. Just think of digging into the soil of a planet millions of miles from home and, better still, to bring some of it back home with you. Our preliminary findings show that the soil on Dooma shows very little difference from that found on Earth. We took samples from many different locations on Dooma and are now working on them in the lab. The planet is rich in minerals and the soil is very fertile and suitable for farming and market gardening. Many varieties of fruit grow in most parts of the planet and the people have developed a very strong farming industry. The Doomans also have a very strong dairy industry. In fact there is one continent that produces mainly dairy products, grain, fruit, and vegetables. The Doomans take very good care of their forests. They harvest areas in rotation and use the whole tree to make an emulsion that can be poured into moulds and hardened. Insulation is included to make a perfect building section in one piece. These sections can then be assembled at the building site in one day. The Doomans kindly provided us with a fully modern home in two days. This process has been put in the hands of your scientists and no doubt will soon be in production here. I also am very grateful to all those who contributed their efforts and expertise to make our project such success.

These reports were very brief and were presented by some very tired astronauts. They would be giving detailed written reports in a few days time. Now they could join their families and enjoy a few days of relaxation in their own Earth homes.

Chapter Seventeen

During the next fifty years there were many questions about the validity of these drastic changes now being put into place. Many were challenged, which was to be expected. However the threat of what would happen if they did not conform soon quelled the arguers. The media kept abreast of the progress of the plans as they were put into practice. One of the most difficult things to overcome was the desire for money. Money had always represented power and this was hard to give up. Those who were used to having money soon found out that not having money leads to a much more relaxing lifestyle without the stress that went along with wealth. These people took over administrative jobs and once they caught on to the goal of a particular project they put everything they could to insure its success.

The Moonbeam crew lived in the same neighborhood and so were able to get together socially on a regular basis. Jim [Groota] had adapted well to life on Earth as he and Betty watched their two children grow up, attend school, and on to university. Jim was very proud to see and be part of the great change taking place.

Bill and Susi now had three children and they were the joy of their lives. One very noticeable change was that there were no young people hanging around on the streets. There were so many things for them to do they had no desire to get into mischief. Another thing that was influencing them was the fact that the focus was on them as the generation that would save our planet. Bill and Susi spent many hours with youth groups promoting sports and other activities. Many weekends were spent camping out with them and teaching them to live with nature. Bill was always happy if he had a fishing rod in his hand and more so when he helped a young boy or girl land his/her first fish. Once in a while Susi yearned for home but she knew what would be involved to go there. Bill said that he would also like to take another trip to Dooma and to take Susi and the children with him. The resource were there to build space craft and, as money was no longer an issue; the chances were very good that this would happen. Special cruises were now available to visit Dooma but the waiting list was long. Of course Bill could get his name on the list as a ship's captain.

Mary Swan was married and had twin boys. She was always ready to cook up a feast for a crew get together. Her husband was an expert on the bar-b-que and was frequently put to work. The boys were fanatic about space travel and for certain wanted to be astronauts. Their father worked at the local spacecraft factory. The boys were frequent visitors to the plant and knew all the new improvements in space travel.

Dr. Tom Morgan worked tirelessly at the hospital working on disease control. He was amazed to see that there wasn't a single case of the common cold reported since the spray operation began. He often consulted with doctors on Dooma by radio and was able to introduce many of the Dooman treatments. The herbs he brought from Dooma were flourishing and were being used on cancer patients with astounding success. He was the only member of the crew that had not married. He said that he was far too busy. He did attend the crew parties when he could.

The new universal language was now in common use because this is what the new generation of children learned from the beginning. Some of the older people didn't bother to learn it but that was no different from the early immigrants to Canada where the old folks never did learn to speak English or French but carried on in their mother tongue. Harry Good, married with four children was very much involved in with schools to change the language and was also involved in having all text books translated into the universal language. He helped to develop a computer program that would translate and print a book at the touch of a key. This meant that any book could be translated. Now many of the children's work books had colored cover depicting pictures of space ships and photographs of the various planets including Dooma.

Through the latest developments in computer communication the children on Earth could now talk to Dooman children. They used the universal language and great friendships grew out of it. Through this medium they could see each other on the computer screen. Through a special web site photographs could be exchanged. There also was the possibility of on-line courting, even though dating would create a bit of a problem. Wasn't Bill's courting with Susi largely done this way?

This close association between the two planets helped to get Earth through the great transition period. Twenty years later would see most of the plans falling into place. There was no sign of one planet feeling superior to the other. There was a silent agreement of co-operation between them. Dooman space ships [UFO'S] were now common visitors to Earth and a regular highway in space was building up, taking visitors to Dooma on vacations. Visitors at both destinations were treated like royalty and the request for such vacations was sky-rocketing. Some of the travelers took extended holidays that lasted several years. Naturally there were a few romances that resulted in marriages.

Through the upbringing of the children unwed couples slowly diminished and marriage vows were honored. Divorce became a thing of the past. Couples aged together and lived a much happier life. The stress of the old ways left them in a relaxed form of life. Nearly all the people went to worship at their local Churches. With a common religion there was no bickering and discrimination within the Church. There was one God, [higher power] that looked over the whole universe. With this in mind, the people on both planets felt a great sense of strength and communion. Isn't this the way mankind is suppose to live?

In the early stages of the big change there were some who had a problem with giving up money. They resorted to bartering with goods. Once they found out that there was no need and they could get whatever they needed when they needed it, it finally sunk in that there was plenty for all and no need for bargain hunting. Certainly, those who had gardens would trade their produce between friends. If a housewife ran out of sugar they thought nothing of going to a neighbor for a cup or two to save running to the store. Besides, it was just another way of getting together for a friendly chat. As there was no monetary value to anything, there was no motive for stealing. There was really no need to lock doors and many folks didn't bother to lock up. They all had their own trinkets and personal things but who would want them. People did have mild arguments but the fights and murders were now unheard of. Mental illness due to stress dropped to only isolated cases.

Of course there were those who were born with mental illness still existed but even those cases were on decline because of the more relaxed lifestyle of the mother. There were still deformities and other natural ailments but modern medical science was able to give these people a close to normal life. A perfect example; A person is blind due to a malfunction of the optic nerve. Through stem cell research the medical team is able to restructure the optic nerve and give sight to the infected eye. In similar fashion the deaf could have their hearing restored. The mute could now talk. These doctors and scientists had a very strong belief in the power of prayer and were often seen to bow their heads before starting a delicate operation. With all the new methods of treating the ill, many pill bottles could be discarded

Another problem that plagued the planet was over population. Restricting the number of children a couple could have was a real hard sell. It was put forward that this was one of the things that would eventually ruin life on Earth. From childhood it was established that a woman should have no more than three children. Continuing with the large families would eventually arrive at a point were Earth could no longer sustain them. Under the new system people could start their families while they were young. There was no need for the mother to work; this was something she could consider after the children were off to college. After all; father was home for half the day and could help with the children.

Chapter Eighteen

This is the final chapter of this book and in closing there are a few personal observations that I feel obligated to make. In taking my readers far into space it makes me realize the immensity of our universe and yet the surface of it has hardly been scratched. The concept of space is beyond the scope of even our imagination. It is certain that there is the possibility of many other populated planets billions of light years beyond our solar system. As human beings we can only speculate what may be discovered in the centuries ahead. In putting these pages together it made me realize the fragility of our dear planet Earth and what senseless efforts we seem to be making to destroy it. Only recently our scientists have stepped up to the plate and informed the world of the danger we are in. Violence has escalated almost to the point of anarchy. Even in our sports the almighty dollar has taken precedence over fair play. As one person expressed, 'I view hockey payers this way. They are overpaid gladiators. One player is given a five year contract of seven million dollars. Is this sport? The fans rave over the game but would come away disappointed if it did not include a few on-ice fights. Violence has spread into some other sports as well. The few that are left are a pleasure to watch or take part in but what are the others teaching our youth? This was another area that needed to be cleaned up.

In these pages I have attempted to show what must be done to rectify our mistakes and try to make a recovery that will bring peace to the Earth. Some will deny the warnings and continue on their destructive paths. Every man, woman, and child on this planet will have to change their thinking and learn to live in peace.

The simplest way to demonstrate how "peace on Earth" could be accomplished was to have a sample to follow. In this case Dooma was this sample. In fiction, time and space has no bounds. The imagination has full rein to be expressed in the written word. I can only hope that this novel will bring an element of entertainment to the reader as well as exposure of what fate may lie ahead. I don't believe that global warming is the threat that is being fed to us. Rather it is a normal cycle such as have been detected over millions of years. What is a much more serious threat is Pollution of the atmosphere, the waterways, and the land itself. Recycling can cut the garbage piles in half. Ways must be found to safely dispose of the other half. Our scientists are working on it and it is hoped that a solution is found before it is too late.

The Doomans were able to overcome another threat to peace and freedom. Hidden behind their religious curtain a large sect of their society infiltrated the general public and rose to be a very dominant form of religion. They had a devastating agenda which was harsh and the intent was to rule the whole planet. The women had no rights; the weak and mentally challenged were slaugh-tered. All non-productive beings were simply done away with. There would be no need for jails because anybody going against their regime was shot with no trial. Before the danger was recognized over twenty five percent of the population had been converted to this so-called Godly agenda. Had it not been caught in time, life on Doo-ma would have been a living Hell. Do we have a similar threat facing us on Earth? We only thought we had put an end to this type of tyranny when we defeated Hitler's Nazi Germany. As I write I see a far more cunning enemy infiltrating societies all over the world. Our heads need to come up out of the sand or we can face the end of free-dom as we see it today.

The sample of Dooma has shown us the importance of child - raising. Children come into the world with an empty *hard drive*. Only proper parenting can load it with appropriate information. The child's mind is like a sponge and the highest level of absorption is in the first five years of life. What better person is there to teach and nurture a child than its mother? As I have mentioned many times, "Watch the animals of the forest". Their young obey or become a meal for a hungry predator. Parenting should be a taught skill like any other endeavor. Of course every parent wants to raise their children in their own way. This is fine to a degree but the basic principles should be estab-lished and maintained. The nature of the child will fol-low the parents and will develop his/her own character.

The ideal situation for the child is to have a devoted couple as parents. The child must have constant love, consistency, and freedom from discord. If possible a baby should be breast fed rather than bottle fed. The modern child is often deprived of these developmental factors because both parents need to work to meet the high cost of living. Once again we can see how the Doomans solved these problems.

Readers will no doubt ask, "What gave the people the incentive to work"? The answer lay in their upbringing. From childhood pride in being a Dooman was always at the fore-front. Part of this was contributing to community in the form of work.. They only worked four hours a day and were generously rewarded in the form of great vacations and other recreational favors. No work; these favors were withheld. There were definitely laws and the people were taught to obey them from a very young age. Enforcement was hardly necessary. During the first years there were problems but as the system fell into place all citizens realized that this was the choice way to live.

Perhaps the most serious flaw in our world are wars and battles; mostly over religious beliefs. If the resources used to fund these wars could be used to feed, shelter, and cloth the whole population, there would be no need to fight over it. Dooma may seem to be paradise and, believe it or not, there is no reason to say that we couldn't have the same here on Earth.

As noted in this story, it will take a lot of effort on the part of every living soul to make this happen. Will it happen? Time will tell.

THE END